P.C. HAWKE
mysteries

THE
E-MAIL
MURDERS

- - - - - - - - -

P.C. HAWKE mysteries

THE E-MAIL MURDERS

- - - - - - - - -

PAUL ZINDEL

Hyperion
New York

To P.C. Hawke's new electronic pals:
Greg, John, Phil, and Colin

Copyright © 2001 by Paul Zindel

Volo and the Volo colophon are trademarks of Disney Enterprises, Inc. All rights reserved. No part of this book may be reproduced or transmitted in any form or by any means, electronic or mechanical, including photocopying, recording, or by any information storage and retrieval system, without written permission from the publisher. For information address Volo Books, 114 Fifth Avenue, New York, New York 10011-5690.

Printed in the United States of America
First Edition
1 3 5 7 9 10 8 6 4 2

The text for this book is set in Janson Text 11.5/15.
Photo of thunderstorm: Don Farrall

Library of Congress Catalog Card Number on file.
ISBN 0-7868-1579-5
Visit www.volobooks.com

Contents

1   Death Online   5

2   The Romantic Corpse   13

3   Kindred Spirits   21

4   Allies and Enemies   33

5   The Cyber Croissant   37

6   Maurice Cardin   43

7   Will the Real Grim Shady Please
    Stand Up?   47

8   Two-Armed Bandit   58

9   The Unexpected   66

10   Van Gogh Was Framed   72

11   Murder à la Mode   79

12   The Last and Most Desperate Meeting   90

13   Hunting Grounds   97

14   A Royal Flush   106

Case #3 began something like this:

There was no way my detective partner, Mackenzie, and I could have known that the death of a young woman on November 4 in the South of France was going to involve us in a freaky and chilling murder case that still gives both of us the willie-jeebies. The basic facts of the case were ghastly enough:

1) Genevieve Blanc, a twenty-eight-year-old waitress in the city of Nice (pronounced NEESS, for those of you who don't speak French), had finished work at a small restaurant on the harbor. She then walked three blocks in the rain to send an e-mail from the local Internet café to her sister Marie in Paris. Genevieve had an Aquafresh smile, medium-length red hair, and a few extra pounds from eating lots of tasty onion pizzas and hot *croque-monsieurs* sold along the docks.

2) Genevieve hadn't noticed someone was staring at her as she came into the Internet café. She booked one of the computers, happily typed in a long e-mail message and sent it off, sipped a café au lait, and nibbled on a croissant before going back out into the night.

3) The pretty young woman also didn't notice she was being followed as she made her way in the rain along the harbor walk before turning down the small dark street to her apartment on the rue Noir. Her first-floor bedroom had glass doors that opened onto a garden overrun with late-blooming hibiscus, yellow lilies, and a lush bed of fragrant roses. She was exhausted from her hard day's

work feeding slabs of garlic bread, steamed mussels, and broiled-fish platters to the demanding tourists. She watched an American sitcom on her small TV, knocked off a glass of red wine from a bottle her parents had sent from Dijon, and went to bed.

4) The police report would later say that somewhere between two and two-thirty in the morning, Genevieve Blanc probably did not hear the sound of someone moving in the garden. She didn't hear the doors of her bedroom opening, nor the thunder or the downpour from the storm outside. More than likely, Genevieve awoke only when she felt the tremendous force of a pillow crushing down on her mouth and nose until all breath was squeezed out of her and she lay dead in the flashes of lightning that tore across the sky.

Now, if it wasn't for this last part of the murder I need to tell you about, I suppose the death of Genevieve Blanc would have simply been lumped in with the other several dozen human slaughter cases that occur along the Côte d'Azur over the course of a year. Mackenzie and I would probably never even have heard about it—but, see, what happened was that the murderer didn't just leave Mademoiselle Blanc's corpse in bed. Whoever did it thoughtfully lifted up Genevieve's body and laid it out carefully on the white tiles of the bathroom floor. The killer meticulously straightened her nightgown about her, gently placed her head on a lace pillow, then combed her red hair and put fresh lipstick and eyebrow pencil on her face. When the police found her, there was a scented candle burning on each side of her head and she held a small bouquet of red roses on her chest.

Little did I (Peter Christopher Hawke, whose notebook this is) and Mackenzie Riggs know that this murder would be the trigger that would eventually pit us against one of the most vicious and dangerous French serial killers of the last twenty years and end with the murderer of Genevieve Blanc trying to snuff the life out of us. This was really a case of life or death—including ours!

Recording the truth and nothing but the truth, I am

C. C. Hawke

(a.k.a. Peter Christopher Hawke)

Death Online

I don't know if you've ever taken a ride in a helicopter, but let me tell you, it's spectacular. And LOUD. I mean, I could see Mackenzie's lips moving, and her thrilled expression, but the only sound was the roar of the rotors.

We raced along the southern coast of France (better known as the Riviera, or the Côte d'Azur) heading toward the Principality of Monaco. Below us lay the blue-green Mediterranean and the golden beaches of the Riviera. Beyond the palm-lined boulevard that hugged the shore, the land rose abruptly. Steep streets zigzagged up sandstone cliffs with luxurious villas perched on their slopes. Our chopper sped past them at eye level, and we could see people relaxing on their balconies, taking in the view.

It was a gorgeous sight, and Mackenzie and I were totally psyched to be there. Her dad, Dr. Dolan Riggs, had been invited to Monaco to be a guest speaker at the International Psychiatric Association Conference, which was being held this year at the Monte Carlo

Grand Hotel, one of the most famous gambling spots on earth.

Dr. Riggs had invited Mackenzie to come with him, since Mrs. Riggs, who is a New York City coroner, had to stay home and work. And Mackenzie, bless her metallic green toenails, had invited her friend and detective partner, me.

"Can you believe this?!" Mackenzie shouted, gesturing out the chopper's window. She was practically jumping up and down—or maybe it was just the motion of the helicopter.

I just nodded and grinned. Vocal cords are a terrible thing to waste, and there was no sense spending the next five days with laryngitis. The helicopter ride from the Nice airport to Monte Carlo was supposed to take only seven minutes—and there would be lots of time to talk once we landed at the hotel, and our ears stopped ringing.

We flew over luxury high-rises, ultramodern shopping centers, marinas with huge yachts lined up port-to-starboard, creatively designed swimming pools, and lots and lots of palm trees.

"What's that?" I yelled to Dr. Riggs, pointing to a narrow, hilly peninsula jutting out into the Mediterranean.

He leaned his considerable bulk toward the window and looked out, stroking his salt-and-pepper beard. "Antibes and Cap Ferrat," he said. I knew from reading the guidebook that those towns were superexclusive, even for this fabulously wealthy corner of the world.

A minute later, he leaned over and pointed out the window again. There, below us, was a formidable fortress sitting atop an impregnable-looking rock, with cliffs on three sides dropping straight into the sea. "Monaco!" he shouted. "Prince Rainier's palace!"

Moments later, our chopper descended, and we landed at a helipad on the roof of the elegant Monte Carlo Grand Hotel.

"Omigod," Mackenzie murmured into my ear as we stepped inside and rode the elevator down six flights. Once we emerged into the impossibly opulent lobby, filled with elegantly dressed people, crystal chandeliers, and lush red carpets, Dr. Riggs went to the front desk to check us in.

"I am in heaven!" Mackenzie declared. "Ooo, look, there's Calvin Klein!"

But it wasn't Calvin at all, just some well-dressed high roller who looked something like him.

"Hey, isn't that Madonna over there?" I said.

The celebrity-spotting went on for a few more minutes; Monaco is a magnet for the world's rich and famous, not to mention a handy tax haven. Then it was time for us to go upstairs.

Our second-floor suite featured a living room with sliding doors that opened onto a balcony, looking out over the beach and the sea. It also had a sofa bed—my home away from home. A small bedroom off to one side would be Mackenzie's. Behind the master bedroom (Dr.

Riggs's, that is) was a second terrace. This one looked out onto the steep mountainside, with its perilously perched villas on concrete stilts and hair-raising roads hugging the edge of the cliff.

"I feel like Princess Grace already!" Mackenzie exclaimed. "Behold, my kingdom!"

"Principality," I corrected.

"Actually, that's France you're looking at," Dr. Riggs corrected *both* of us. "Monaco stops about five blocks inland, and hugs the water for about three miles from one end to the other. The border to France is wide open on either side, but don't go straying too far while I'm at the conference."

"We won't," I assured him.

"No way," Mac agreed. "I know what you're thinking, Daddy. We're on vacation from tracking down criminals. Totally. Sunbathing and sight-seeing, and that's it, I promise."

Dr. Riggs, of course, was well aware of our penchant for getting into dangerous scrapes in pursuit of justice. "Good," he said, looking relieved. "Now, I've got a luncheon to attend in half an hour. I suggest you two get out and walk around the place. You can see it all on foot or you can use the trains. They're easy to figure out between here and Nice, and all points in between. Cannes is not too far away either, in case you're interested."

"Cannes? Where they have the film festival?" I asked.

"That's right," he said.

"Cool!" Mackenzie said, rubbing her hands together. "I could get into some stargazing."

"Maybe you ought to start by checking out the Prince's palace," he suggested. "It's in the cliff area known as 'the Rock.' So's the Oceanographic Institute. It's one of the world's greatest, and it's got an amazing aquarium."

"Sounds good," I said. "What about unpacking, though?"

"Later for that!" Mackenzie said, pulling me away from the balcony railing and back inside the suite. "We've only got five days here. Let's get started *now*."

We strolled through the narrow streets of Monaco's Old Town, snapping lots of pictures to show our friends back at Westside School. "I can't wait to show these to the kids back at Westside," Mackenzie said, taking a shot of café awnings and tables with umbrellas. "Not that I'm into bragging about where I've been, of course. It's just fun to watch your friends drool."

"Ah, yes, but we have not yet even sampled ze food," I reminded her in my best French accent—which is pretty good, if I say so myself, for a guy who speaks no French.

"I wonder if Monac–Mon . . . what do they call themselves?"

"Monegasques," I said.

"Monegasques? That's funky. Monegasques . . ." Mackenzie repeated. "I wonder if they eat the same food as the French. . . ."

"According to the guidebook," I read, "'the culture is the same as in France.' I guess that would include the cuisine. Speaking of which, this café looks promising."

Mackenzie agreed, so we sat down at an outdoor table to have a bite of *déjeuner* (that's lunch, to you).

"Hey, check this out," I said, scanning the front page of an English-language newsaper someone had left behind. "Did you know they have serial killers in France, too?"

"Really?" Mackenzie slid her chair over so we could read the article together. We might have been on vacation, but that didn't mean we weren't interested. If it concerns crime, it concerns us.

The article was about a totally bizarre killer known as "Cyrano." He had named himself, it seemed, after the fictional romantic hero Cyrano de Bergerac. And certainly, this Cyrano had a touch of the romantic. He had a very unique modus operandi. He attacked only redheads, smothered them with a pillow, and left them neatly laid out on the bathroom floor in full makeup, flanked by aromatic candles, and clutching red roses to their chests. The killer always targeted his victims via e-mail, striking up a correspondence with them. The last e-mail from Cyrano to the victim always read, *Les roses pour vous. Toujours* [Roses for you. Forever], *Cyrano.*"

Romantic or not, he'd already killed seventeen women in Paris. And then, just one week ago, he'd struck again in Nice.

"So close to here," I said. "Hey, Mac, do you think—?"

"No!" Mackenzie stopped me. "P.C., don't even go there. We are on vacation."

"I know. Still, we've never hunted a serial killer before."

"I know," she sighed. "But this isn't America, P.C. We don't know how things work here."

"We weren't exactly L.A. natives, either," I pointed out, reminding her of our last case, which had ended with the death of a would-be murderer, and with us narrowly escaping the same fate.

We ordered two French-style ham-and-cheese sandwiches, called *croque-monsieurs*. While we waited for our food to arrive, we studied the article some more.

"Creepy," Mackenzie breathed, once we'd taken in all the gory details. "It gives me the shivers just thinking about it."

"I wouldn't go coloring my hair red, if I were you," I told her. Mackenzie has long blond hair, and it looks really good on her, but I wouldn't put it past her to fool around with a new look, just for fun.

"Ha-ha," she said, not amused. "Just think, though. Cyrano could be anybody—that guy over there, for instance." She nodded toward a fat, bald man who looked like a banker, sitting at one of the other tables.

"And how will we ever know if we don't investigate? We could at least go out to the scene of the crime. Your dad said it was easy to get around this place."

"Stop, P.C.," she said warningly, but I could tell I was getting to her.

"We could rent a couple of scooters and drive over there."

"Forget it!" she said quickly. We had nearly lost our lives on scooters in L.A., speeding down a cliffside road just like the ones here.

"Ah, well," I said, biting down on my sandwich. "I guess we'll just have to let Cyrano get off scot-free."

Mackenzie glared at me. "The bottom line is, I promised my dad." She counted out some French francs (which are used as money in Monaco) and paid for lunch. "And so did you, P.C. A promise is a promise."

"You're right," I said. She frowned when I tore out the Cyrano article and put it in my wallet.

But we spent the rest of that day as tourists: checking out the gilded halls and bedrooms on the palace tour, tanning on a stony beach, and swimming in the blue waters that give the Côte d'Azur its name. We fell asleep right after a humongous dinner of garlic shrimp and chocolate mousse at our hotel.

All in all, it had been a blissful, lollygagging day. And I guess it was a good thing we rested up, because the next morning, we woke up to a fresh, chilling Cyrano murder right smack in our own hotel!

2

The Romantic Corpse

The police sirens woke us up; it sounded like dozens of them. With all the rich and famous people who hang out there, Monaco is on constant security alert, which makes it usually one of the safest places on earth.

Mackenzie, Dr. Riggs, and I were up and dressed by the time the police banged on the door of our suite. There were four of them standing there. One, a short, middle-aged man with handsome features and kind eyes, stepped forward and said, "Dr. Riggs?"

"That's me," Mackenzie's father said.

"You are the head of the New York Society of Psychoanalysts?"

"Yes . . ."

"I am Inspector LeSeur," the officer said, giving Dr. Riggs a little bow of the head. "There has been a most unfortunate incident involving one of your colleagues, I'm afraid. If you will please come with us, monsieur."

He led the way down the hall to the elevators, and the rest of us followed. LeSeur had a French accent, but his English was pretty fluent as he explained that one of the psychoanalysts attending the conference had been grue-somely murdered. "The victim's name is Dr. Harriet Epstein-Hopper," he said.

"My God!" Dr. Riggs exclaimed. "Harriet? I know her quite well, Inspector. And her husband, too, Dr. Richard Hopper."

"Yes, I understand they are both quite eminent. But come, see for yourself what we have found."

The elevator stopped at the third floor, and we got out. LeSeur led us down the corridor toward the crime scene. Police were everywhere, pouring over suite 307, where the murder had taken place, inspecting the suites on either side, the bank of elevators, and the terraces off the rooms. Teams of uniformed men and women searched for clues, dusted for fingerprints, and inter-viewed other shocked and puzzled hotel guests on the floor.

LeSeur was clearly in command of the whole opera-tion. He gave orders in French, which I won't translate, because I can't. Unfortunately, I take Spanish and German in school.

To tell you the truth, even if I spoke French, it wouldn't have made much difference. Everyone was talking like machine guns, and at the same time; it would have been impossible to tell what they were saying.

Dr. Riggs was busy talking to the police and no one was paying much attention to Mackenzie or me. We exchanged a nod, and went into action. Mac edged her way forward and into the suite, trying to look as casual as possible, so no one would notice her and shoo her away.

As for me, I decided to tag along with LeSeur as he made the rounds, going from person to person and checking on their progress. He held a walkie-talkie in one hand, and spoke into it in rapid-fire French. I got frustrated pretty quickly, being right there but not understanding a word anybody was saying, but after a couple of minutes my attention was diverted by a girl— okay, a *beautiful* girl—who seemed to be trailing LeSeur, just as I was doing.

She had wavy red hair down to her shoulder blades, delicate hands, and a thin red-and-white cane. Her fascinatingly large blue eyes stared into space, not as though they were sightless, but as if they saw things no one else could see.

She kept close to LeSeur, listening to everything he said with her head cocked to one side. At one point, she tugged on LeSeur's coat, and said, *"Papa?"* He leaned toward her, and she whispered something in his ear. LeSeur listened, nodded slowly, then said something to his subordinates, as if she'd given him the idea.

So, the babe of a blind girl was LeSeur's daughter. I wondered if she spoke any English; maybe I could get her to translate for me. *"Bonjour,"* I said, coming up alongside her and tossing off one of the five French words I know.

"*Bonjour*," she said, giving me a nod and a charming smile. "I am Juliette," she continued in English.

Juliette. Too bad my name wasn't Romeo. "My name's P.C.," I said.

She laughed. "*Pee-See?* That is a name I never hear."

"It stands for Peter Christopher," I told her.

"Ah!" she said. "You stay at the hotel, P.C.?"

"Yes. I'm here with my friend Mackenzie and her dad, who's speaking at the conference. You're the inspector's daughter, huh?" I asked.

"Yes, Papa is the chief police inspector here in Monte Carlo." She emphasized the second syllable: pa-PAH.

"I couldn't help noticing—were you giving your dad *suggestions*?"

"*Oui*," she admitted. "I sometimes perceive things that seeing people do not. And I hope to be a detective also someday."

"My friend Mackenzie and I have solved a couple of cases ourselves," I replied, trying to be cool.

"Hey, P.C. I just got busted by one scary police-woman with a mustache. . . ." Mackenzie stopped, suddenly noticing I wasn't alone. "Um, *bonjour*," she said.

"This," I said, "is Juliette. She speaks English. Juliette LeSeur, meet Mackenzie Riggs."

"Hi, Mackenzie," Juliette said.

"LeSeur? Is your dad—?"

"He is the detective, yes."

Mackenzie immediately locked in on Juliette. "Listen,

16

do you have any idea what's going on? All we know is that Dr. Epstein-Hopper was murdered."

"I know a little," Juliette said. "She was killed not long ago—the coroner thinks between six-thirty and seven A.M. Suffocation. They found her on the floor of the bathroom, just like the other victims of the killer Cyrano. You know of him?"

"We read something in the paper," I told her.

"She have red hair, the dead lady," Juliette said, fingering her own hair. "*Comme ça*, only more short. And she have her head on a pillow, with candles burning on each side of her face, and red roses in her hands."

I was about to fish the article out of my back pocket when the police brought in the victim's husband. Dr. Richard Hopper looked to be in bad shape. He was clearly devastated: they must have given him the news just moments before. He looked to be around fifty. He was wearing running shorts, a New York Athletic Club T-shirt, and white Nike running shoes. Obviously, he'd just come back from his morning jog. I checked my watch. It was ten minutes to eight.

"It is the husband, no?" Juliette asked us.

"Yes," Mackenzie whispered.

"How pitiful he sounds, poor man!"

The police brought Dr. Hopper into his suite, and sat him down on a sofa. He was bawling and moaning, shaking his head in disbelief. He wanted to see his wife, but they weren't letting him anywhere near the bathroom. There were still police photographers in there with the body.

"Can you tell us, monsieur, exactly what happened from the time you woke up this morning?" Inspector LeSeur asked him.

"I got up around five-fifteen for my morning run," he managed to say. "I put on my running clothes, and . . . I guess I left the hotel around five-thirty . . . Oh, God . . . poor Harriet!"

"And you were running all this time?" the inspector asked gently.

"Yes. I mean, no. I . . . I stopped afterward at a café for coffee and a brioche."

"And the name of this café?"

Dr. Hopper thought a moment. "The Corniche," he said. " At least, I think that was what it was called."

"And someone there would remember you?"

"I would think so."

"But you ordered breakfast via room service, monsieur?" LeSeur asked, looking at the untouched tray containing covered dishes and a bud vase with a single sprig of lavender. The inspector lifted the dishes and examined the food.

"I ordered it last night for Harriet. She was still at the blackjack tables. It was after midnight. I was tired. I knew I'd be up and out early, so I filled out the room service form and left it on the doorknob before I went to bed. I don't know what time Harriet came in, but she was there, sleeping, when I woke up this morning."

"I see. It was the waiter who discovered your wife's body when he arrived with the tray at seven-fifteen. When no one answered his knock, he opened the door with his passkey to leave the breakfast tray in the sitting room and saw your wife's body on the bathroom floor."

"Harriet!" Dr. Hopper cried.

"I am so sorry, monsieur," LeSeur said again. "It is a terrible loss. If you would like to see her now."

Juliette, Mackenzie, and I backed out the door and retreated to a quiet corner of the hallway. "Okay," I said. "So, Juliette, about Cyrano . . ."

"My father, he was investigating this case in Paris last year," she began. "He transfer here only six months before now. The French and Monegasque police, they have cooperation agreements. You understand?"

"Is that why he's in charge of this investigation?" I asked.

"*Oui*. Because he knows so much about Cyrano," Juliette said.

"So, that would mean you know something about it, too?" Mackenzie prodded.

Juliette lit up. "Oh, yes, I know many things about the vicious Cyrano. Also there are the computer files in my father's office. I cannot read them, of course." She tapped the floor with her cane.

"We could read them to you!" I said. "Can we get in and see those files?"

"Of course!" Juliette said. "I sometimes do work with Papa, so if I say you are my friends, it will be okay."

"Cool!" Mackenzie said excitedly.

Suddenly there was a commotion as a young, muscular man with long, flowing dark hair was led down the hall. He shouted at the two policemen who had him by the arms, and tried to wrestle free of them.

"What's going on? What's he shouting?" I asked Juliette.

"The police have a suspect!" she said, clutching me by the arm. "Let's *go*!"

3

Kindred Spirits

Inspector LeSeur spoke to the suspect. "Are you Tomas Milano?"

"Yes," Milano said gruffly. He looked to be in his late twenties. His deep-set eyes kept shifting left and right, as if looking for a way out. He suddenly shouted in Italian-accented English, "I protest this brutal treatment! I am innocent! I will call my lawyer!"

LeSeur ignored his outburst. "You were seen leaving the casino with the deceased around two A.M., monsieur."

"*Si*," Milano agreed. "I make the lady's acquaintance in the casino. We play blackjack. Then I escort her to her suite, and we say good night. *Basta, finito!* And now you say I kill her? It is an outrage!"

In my experience, nobody protests his innocence more than the guilty party.

Anyway, LeSeur wasn't through grilling him. "You are well known in this hotel, monsieur," he told Milano. "As I understand it, your 'racket' is to charm older, rich ladies, and then relieve them of their money or jewelry, *n'est-ce pas?*"

"It is of murder you accuse me, *Ispettore*," Milano shot back. "Of this, I am innocent. If you wish to discuss my livelihood, that is another matter."

I have to say, Tomas Milano had a lot of nerve. I could see how some women might fall for him, with his "passionate Italian" act. Had Milano cast his spell over Dr. Hopper's wife? And had he then entered her suite and murdered her while her husband was out jogging?

LeSeur gave Milano a doubtful look. "We already know your modus operandi, monsieur. You masquerade as a 'protector' of lady winners, claiming the casino staff has assigned you to that job."

"*Ispettore*, since you seem to know all about me, why bother to ask questions?" Tomas Milano said. He brushed back his hair and stroked his eyebrows, striking a casual pose on the sofa.

LeSeur ignored Milano's taunting tone, and went on. "Casino surveillance cameras show that you escorted Madame Epstein-Hopper back to her room at precisely two-oh-five A.M."

"Of this, I am guilty as charged, *signore*." Milano gave LeSeur a smile.

"Dr. Epstein-Hopper had won a lot of money at the blackjack tables," LeSeur continued. "She was a wealthy woman, who wore expensive jewelry; her Cartier watch is now missing." He glared at Milano. "Your motive for murder was robbery, monsieur. You made sure the door was unlocked at two A.M. Then you returned between six and seven, while her husband was out jogging. You killed her à la Cyrano, to throw the police off your track. Then you took her watch and made your escape."

Milano chuckled. "At the time of the murder, I was with my girlfriend Nicole at her apartment on rue Grimaldi. But you already know this, since it is where your men picked me up."

LeSeur looked furious. "Very well, monsieur, you may go for now. But I warn you, do not try to leave the principality. My people will be watching you."

"I would not dream of leaving, *Ispettore*," Milano assured him with a little bow. "I like it here. So many nice ladies, you know." He strolled out of the suite, clearly pleased with himself.

"Jeez," Mackenzie said under her breath as he walked by us. "Smooth operator!"

"I'll say," I agreed. "Do you think it was him?"

"I don't know," Mackenzie replied. "His girlfriend would certainly lie for him if he asked her for an alibi."

"But what about the surveillance cameras?" I said.

It was Juliette who answered. "The hallways are not the only way into the guest rooms. They can also be entered from adjoining suites."

"True, but only if the door is unlocked from both sides," I said. "That would mean the victim opened the door to her attacker willingly."

"Which she might have done for Tomas," Mackenzie suggested.

"Or someone else she knew," I said. "Hey! Why don't we go to the front desk and find out who has the rooms on either side of this one?"

"I want to check something out first," Mackenzie said, turning and sneaking back into the suite. Ten seconds later, she was hustled out again by the same angry policewoman who'd removed her the first time. But Mackenzie was smiling. *"Les roses pour vous. Toujours, Cyrano,"* she said. "It was right there on the screen, just as I thought it would be."

"It's Cyrano, all right," Juliette said.

"We've never tracked a serial killer before," Mackenzie told Juliette.

I could tell Mac was up for the chase, and that she'd totally forgotten her father's warning about us staying off the case. That was okay with me. The beach would have to wait.

"Tell us everything you know about Cyrano," I said to Juliette. The police were cordoning off the suite, and those on either side, with yellow police tape, the universally understood KEEP OUT sign.

"I know that my papa, he checked out all the e-mails. But in Paris, the e-mail from Cyrano came from different sources, ones with a lot of users. The investigation there goes very slowly."

"What about the latest victims?" I asked.

"We can check at the police station."

"You said Milano didn't seem like the Cyrano type,"

Mackenzie said to Juliette. "Why not?"

"My papa, he says Cyrano is a loner. Like most serial killers."

"Sure doesn't sound like Milano," I said. "Okay, what else can you tell us?"

"I know he likes to spray perfume on the victims," Juliette replied. "This you do not read in the newspapers, but I discover it myself at a crime scene in Paris. The smell of tuberose was there. Very faint, but I smelled it."

I'd never even heard of tuberose, and neither had Mackenzie. But this girl had smelled it, and identified it, by just a faint trace of the scent.

"Tuberose is used in perfumes," Juliette explained. "Not so much now, but before, maybe twenty, thirty years ago. It is a very unusual scent. Papa is trying to track down the source of the perfume. Maybe he will discover who buys it. I think maybe soon, we will have a good clue from this. Not many men would buy a perfume with tuberose."

"Good!" Mackenzie said. "It's going to be a short list."

"Yes. But as I say, the French police, they work so slowly! And in Monaco, it is even worse. Thorough, yes. Fast, no."

"Then they need us!" I said. "If we can dig up or piece together something crucial the police have missed or didn't get to, maybe we can catch Cyrano before he commits his next murder."

I have to admit, when I said that, I was looking at Juliette's long, undulating, red hair. She was definitely in the high-risk category.

"You know what?" Mackenzie said. "I just thought of something. One of the shrinks at this conference is an expert in serial killers."

"No kidding? Who?" I asked.

"My dad was talking about her the other day. Francine somebody-or-other. She's scheduled to give one of the speeches here."

"We could check the conference brochure," I said.

We escorted Juliette back up to our suite, where we checked Dr. Riggs's copy of the conference events. Juliette called the hotel's front desk, but they wouldn't give out any room numbers. We had to schlepp back down to the lobby, and it took a good half hour before we could get anyone to tell us anything. Finally, Juliette dropped her father's name, and we found something very curious indeed. Dr. Francine White, the serial killer expert in question, had been in suite 306—right next door to the Hoppers' suite! But since the police had sealed off the neighboring suites for the investigation, Dr. White had been moved to suite 542 in the hotel's other wing.

As we approached suite 542, we saw that the door was slightly ajar. Sneaking up to it, we saw that Dr. White was inside, hanging up clothes from her suitcase, which lay open on the bed. Someone else was in there, too:

none other than a now less-than-weepy Dr. Richard Hopper! The two of them were engaged in a hushed— and what looked like a very intimate—conversation.

"Richard, please!" Dr. White was saying.

Francine White was younger than Richard Hopper by maybe ten years or so. She wasn't exactly a great beauty, but not a bowwow either. Her voice was rough and deep, with a determined edge to it. Next to her, Hopper seemed like a psycho wimp.

"I'm going to ask that the conference proceed as scheduled," he said, looking down at the carpet. "Harriet would have wanted it that way."

"Yes, I guess that much is true," Dr. White agreed.

"And furthermore, I'm going to suggest that you take Harriet's place as keynote speaker." Dr. White started to protest, but he stopped her with a raised hand. "I don't care how it looks. It's only right."

"Wake up and smell the coffee!" she growled. "We're murder suspects, both of us! I had the suite next door to yours, for goodness' sake! But I don't happen to have a convenient alibi like yours."

I glanced briefly at Juliette. She was paying rapt attention.

"I suppose you're right," Hopper said. "Well, then, I suppose I could ask Dr. Piatkowski to take over Harriet's slot."

"You do that," she told him. "And stay away from me for a while."

To our shock, Dr. Hopper kissed her on the lips, and left via the connecting door to the adjoining suite.

Mackenzie glanced over at me with a look of total disbelief.

"He kissed her," she whispered to Juliette.

"Talk about weird," I said. I cleared my throat and knocked on the door of the suite. Dr. White came forward, her face a sickly white. Clearly she was worried that we had overheard her conversation with Hopper. "Yes?" she said.

We introduced ourselves. Juliette and I let Mackenzie take the lead. Once Dr. White realized she was Dr. Riggs's daughter, she seemed a little more at ease. We decided not to mention just yet that Juliette was Inspector LeSeur's daughter. Mackenzie's next question, though, seemed to shake Dr. White up.

"We were hoping you could tell us about serial killers, and about Cyrano in particular?" Mackenzie asked.

"Why would you want to know that?" Dr. White's voice had dropped an octave deeper, as if she were trying to frighten us into not being too nosy.

"Mackenzie and I go to Westside School in Manhattan," I cut in, "and we thought we might do our junior-year research paper on killers like Cyrano. We might throw in a few of the other famous American serial killer guys, too, like Ted Bundy and a couple of the others."

Juliette piped up. "I might do such a paper for my

school here in Monaco," she said, accentuating her French accent.

Mac gave a final gush. "We would just like a few pointers," she said. "Why does someone like Cyrano do what he does? It's like he's got a whole ritual thing going."

A softening crept into Dr. White's eyes, as if she had really bought our "Oh, we're just silly little students ready to worship at your feet" routine. Mackenzie and I have used that approach on a lot of uptight adults we want to grill.

"Understanding Cyrano is easy," Dr. White said. She glanced over to her work tables. "Come look at what I've been pulling up on my computer."

"We know you're going to give a speech at the conference," I said.

"Yes." She actually smiled, but still looked a teensy bit like a prison matron who might get a kick out of watching a good execution. "You can get an advance look at my lecture. After what's happened, I've decided to shift its focus entirely onto this Cyrano horror."

The files were in text-only format, most likely downloaded from Dr. White's Web site. I scrolled slowly through the document while Mackenzie read aloud so Juliette could hear:

"'Serial killers are not your usual suspects. They are incredibly complicated in their backgrounds and motivations. Cyrano was likely an abused child—abused by his mother, and perhaps also by his father. He may have expressed his early anguish by killing family pets, or local stray animals. Like the fictional Cyrano, he would most likely be a large, powerful man, who hides behind others. Perhaps he also has a physical deformity like Cyrano's. At any rate, he is likely the kind of man girls laugh at, or shun, as his mother did. It might well be that his mother was tall, and had long, red hair, like his victims.'"

"If you'll forgive my saying so," I ventured, "this all seems like a kind of simplified profile."

"Of course it's simplified!" Dr. White retorted. "No one knows who Cyrano is. But put it this way, when Interpol wants a profile of a serial killer, they always come to me for my *simpleness*." Her eyes looked as if she wanted to slap me.

"Sorry," I said. "I didn't mean to insult you."

"Never mind." She waved me off. "But I'm afraid I'm going to have to cut this short. I have to leave for an appointment."

"Of course," Mackenzie said, taking over the scrolling. She kept reading: "'He's killed tall, long red-haired women for years. He kills to create the event of love and tenderness his subconscious cries out for. He creates his perfect date: his ideal mother. He makes his chosen woman behave exactly as he wishes, ultimately by rendering her dead through suffocation with a pillow. Then he lays her out peacefully, holding a rose and surrounded by romantic candlelight, with the pillow under her head. This ritual is the only way he can achieve his fantasy of being loved by a woman. This is someone who wants women to be sweet, gentle. He wants women to let him control them. . . .'"

Dr. White shot out a finger and shut off the computer. She ushered us out and we headed back to our suite to do some more unpacking, and to go over what we'd learned so far. Juliette stayed with us. "Okay, we have a murder of an eminent psychiatrist," Mackenzie began as we got to work putting our clothes in drawers and on hangers. "A murder that fits the profile of one by a serial killer named Cyrano."

"Not to mention the other killing nearby in Nice," Juliette reminded us.

Mackenzie nodded. "And now we have some idea of what Cyrano might be like."

"But we also have two people who knew the dead woman, and had a motive to kill her," I pointed out. "And then there's Tomas Milano. Whether or not he's Cyrano, he certainly knew the deceased, and might have tried to rob her. Maybe she woke up to him breaking into her suite, and he killed her, then dressed the crime scene up to make it look like a Cyrano murder."

"Don't forget the tuberose," Juliette said. "You know, I didn't smell any in the suite this morning."

"This is a totally freaky case," Mackenzie said, sighing. "So many surreal possibilities."

"We can start by going with Juliette to the police station and looking over their files. That would help."

"I think it would," Juliette said.

"Right. And what about the casino's surveillance videotapes of the hallway?" I mentioned. "We should find out what was on them."

"Or what *wasn't*," Mackenzie agreed. "And what about the e-mail to Dr. Epstein-Hopper? Have the police tracked down the source?"

Dr. Riggs appeared in the doorway, looking stressed and on overload. "Such a horrible thing to happen! Poor Harriet; poor Richard," he said. Suddenly he was aware of Juliette's presence. "Oh, hello."

"*Bonjour*," she replied, offering her hand for him to shake. "I am Juliette. Police Inspector LeSeur is my father."

Dr. Riggs looked over at Mac and me, a suspicious expression on his face. "I hope this doesn't mean you kids have decided to get involved in this thing."

"No, Daddy," Mackenzie lied.

"Remember, you promised," he reminded us.

"We remember," I said, which at least was true.

"You're to stay out of this, you understand me?"

"We understand," Mackenzie and I said stereophonically. We did understand. We just sort of knew there wasn't a chance we were going to drop this case. Not in a zillion years.

Allies and Enemies

Monaco's Central Police Station is an imposing building, fronted with white columns at the head of a flight of stone steps. Inside, all was quiet, unlike your typical American police station. Most of the work was being done behind closed doors: in the labs, the hall of records, the morgue. The jail cells, Juliette told us, were two stories underground. If the prisoners were making a racket, we couldn't hear them.

Juliette led us past the uniformed receptionist and down the hall to her father's office. LeSeur was still at the crime scene, so it was the perfect time to log on to the Cyrano files on his computer. Juliette knew all the passwords, and soon we were cross-checking all the Cyrano murders, comparing them, and picking out the differences. One item in particular caught my attention. "All the victims had long red hair, except for the last two. Genevieve Blanc and Dr. Epstein-Hopper both had fairly short haircuts."

"Do you think that *means* anything?" Mackenzie asked. "He could have just had a hard time finding someone exactly right."

"I don't know. Maybe Cyrano's tastes are changing," I commented. "Or maybe we're dealing with a copycat killer here."

I noticed an 8 x 10 of a striking woman with long red hair on LeSeur's desk. "Is this your mother?" I asked Juliette.

"*Oui*," Juliette answered proudly. "She is a model. She is very beautiful, no?"

"Very," Mackenzie agreed, taking over the computer.

"Funny how both you and your mother fit the profile," I said.

"This is why my papa is so interested in Cyrano, I think. But I am not afraid," Juliette insisted. "I can take care of myself."

"Hey, check this out," Mackenzie said. "Many of the e-mails were sent from one of the Sorbonne university libraries in Paris."

"*Oui*," Juliette agreed, "but it would be easy to fake a student or faculty ID to use those computers. It's like a factory. You can sit there all day."

"How about the e-mail to Genevieve Blanc, though?" Mac said. She punched a few buttons, and stared at the screen, waiting for the information to appear.

"Meanwhile, what about the surveillance videos?" I asked. "Can we look at them?"

Juliette and Mac went to check on the status of the tapes in the lab on the second floor. While they were gone, I studied the Genevieve Blanc file. I retraced her final hours, referring to a wall map of Nice behind LeSeur's desk.

There were three points of interest: the Madeleine Restaurant on the boulevard, where she'd worked the dinner shift that evening; the Cyber Croissant, a local Internet café where she'd stopped after work to e-mail her sister in Paris; and her apartment on the rue Noir, just off the boulevard, where she'd gone home to bed—and where she'd met her gruesome end.

I wanted to check out all those places. It was clear to me that Dr. Harriet Epstein-Hopper's death was connected to Genevieve's, since they were the only two murders that had happened in the area. It was impossible to examine the crime scene at the hotel: the police would still be swarming all over it. But they were long done with Genevieve's murder, having already filed it away under "Cyrano."

The girls returned, excited by fresh news. "The photo lab technicians say the tapes confirmed Dr. Hopper's alibi," Mackenzie told me. "He left at five-thirty, and didn't return until we saw him brought in at seven-fifty."

"And Tomas, he bring her back at two-oh-five A.M., just as he said—and he doesn't come back again," Juliette added.

"There was no sign of Cyrano either," said Mackenzie. "Nothing suspicious on any of the tapes at all."

"There was more than one tape?" I asked.

"*Oui*," Juliette said. "One from one A.M. to four A.M., one from four A.M. to seven A.M., the third from seven A.M. to ten A.M., although of course it was stopped at seven-forty-five, when the police took it away. No one comes near the suite after Tomas, until Dr. Hopper goes out at five-thirty."

"What about the candles, the roses, and all the ritual props?" I asked. "Are the police running down the sources of those items?"

"*Oui*, slowly, slowly," Juliette said.

Just then, the computer stopped searching the source of the e-mail to Genevieve Blanc, and coughed up a name.

"Hey, check this out!" I said, staring at the screen. "Cyrano's e-mail came from the Cyber Croissant. That's the same café Genevieve was in that night!"

"What are you saying?" Mackenzie asked.

I pointed out the Cyber Croissant's location on the map. "There's something about Nice that *ain't* so nice."

5

The Cyber Croissant

We thought for a moment about renting scooters again, as we had in L.A. But of course, there was Juliette to think of. So in the end, we settled for the train, which runs along the base of the mountain that separates Monaco from France.

It took us only fifteen minutes to get to Nice. We made the Madeleine restaurant where Genevieve Blanc had worked our first stop, a brief one, since there wasn't any interesting info there, then retraced Genevieve's route on that fatal, stormy night.

The conditions couldn't have been more different: afternoon sunshine made the harbor crescent look like a dazzling crown. The Cyber Croissant was three blocks up from the beach promenade, in the Vieux (Old) Nice area. It was crowded at this hour, mostly with trendy-looking young people, although it seemed every five minutes some ambulance came screaming by. Their pulsing sirens sounded just like the kind you hear in gangster movies, but it was a reminder that Nice is a place where a lot of older, well-heeled people come to hole up in rest homes and die. I figured the emergency rooms at the hospitals there must all be as busy as Burger Kings on a free-French-fries day in New York.

The Cyber Croissant looked like a sixties San Francisco hangout, with psychedelic posters of Jim Morrison and an espresso bar with muffins where you could just tell that a mob of giant Riviera cockroaches could have a ball. There didn't seem to be a free computer in the place, so we sidled up to a spot in front of a rack of coffee cups.

The guy behind the bar was an aging French-hippy type. He was fashionably dressed, but had long, unkempt salt-and-pepper hair, and an almost sadistic-looking leer. "It is I," he told us when we asked for the café's owner. "You can call me Pierre."

"I'm P.C." I reached out to shake his hand. "This is Mackenzie, and Juliette."

"P.C., you like some café au lait? And would *les belles demoiselles* like something?" he asked, looking from Mackenzie to Juliette and back again.

"Whatever the ladies want," I said, trying to be cool and nonchalant. I pulled some French francs out of my pocket and slapped them down on the bar. "On me."

"*Eh, bien, monsieur!*" Pierre said, giving me a revolting fake smile. "You are, how you say, the big shot! I find you a computer soon, okay?"

"Actually," Mackenzie said, "we came in because of the Cyrano murder."

Pierre's expression darkened. "Ah, that," he said bitterly. "Is good for business—the tourists, they come to see the place where Genevieve Blanc was last seen. But the police, I do not like them around so much."

"It must be terrible!" Mackenzie said sympathetically. "The police snooping around, asking offensive questions of a man like yourself!"

"You understand exactly," Pierre said.

"Okay. I guess I'll take a café au lait when you have a chance," I said. I figured it couldn't hurt the investigation to spend a few francs at the guy's café. Mackenzie and Juliette asked for espressos.

We chatted while Pierre got our drinks. When he returned, Mac went in for the grill kill. "Hey, cool shirt," she said, running a finger up and down his sleeve. "Is it Armani?"

"*Oui*, Armani," Pierre grinned. "You like?"

"*Très chic*," Mackenzie said. "Few men really know how to dress. I like the slacks, too."

Pierre picked an imaginary piece of lint off his pants. I rolled my eyes, not being big on fashion. But Mackenzie knew what she was doing.

"The girl who was murdered, did you talk to her?" Mac asked.

Pierre shrugged. "I talk to so many, but I remember only a few." He looked from Juliette to Mackenzie, as if to say he would not soon forget either of them. "But no, this poor girl, I do not remember her. Not until the police show me her picture. Then I remember she was sitting alone, over there by the window." He pointed to a workstation near the door, where two noisy boys were maneuvering themselves through Zelda World.

"And she was here for how long?" Juliette asked.

"One half-hour, maybe," Pierre said with a shrug.

"She left alone?" Mac asked.

"*Oui*, alone," Pierre confirmed. "I think so. It is hard to remember."

"You told the police she left alone," I reminded him.

"*Oui*," he said. "The police, they made me nervous, but just now, I remind myself something . . ."

"What?" Mackenzie asked.

"Massimo," he said.

"Massimo?" we all repeated.

"*Oui.* You say something about my clothes, and now I remember. Just after the young lady leave the café, I look up from my work, and I notice a pair of black Massimo trousers going out into the rain."

"How long after she left?" I pressed.

"One minute, maybe two."

"Could he have followed her? Stalked her?" Mac asked. To this, Pierre only shrugged.

Juliette shot a spray of rapid-fire French at him. Then she repeated in English, "Is there anything else you remember?"

"Let me think," Pierre said. "Yes, I remember now. He sat over *there*." He pointed to his left, indicating a corner of the café with a perfect view of the door, but out of sight of the bar. "He was there a long time before the girl come in, but the café, it was so busy that night. So many people come in out of the storm."

"You must have gotten a good look at him," Mackenzie said.

"He send e-mail, he order . . . ah! A double espresso and chocolate croissant! And he pay in cash. Large bills. Also, he have dark hair. Long."

"Milano!" Mackenzie breathed.

"Could have been a wig, too," I pointed out. "Anything else about the way he looked?"

"He was wearing an overcoat with the collar turned up, and a baseball cap that cover his face. I don't pay so much attention, so I don't notice how old, or what he look like. But when he leave, I notice the trousers, because they are *très* hot. Sports pockets on the side." Pierre shook his head in wonderment. "It is amazing that a man with such taste would stay at such a cheap hotel."

I blinked in astonishment. "Hotel? What hotel?"

"Ah, this too, the police make me so nervous I forget. This man, he have with him a small writing pad. I see it, and I remember what it say: *Le Bec Zinc*."

"Le Bec Zinc?" I repeated, flummoxed.

"It is a cheap pension up beyond the train station. Maybe he is there now, I do not know. It is what you Americans call a flophouse."

"Okay, guys," I said. "We're out! Thank you so much, Pierre. Believe me, when Cyrano is caught, your place will be the hottest café in town."

Mackenzie was already heading for the door.

"*Au revoir,*" Juliette told him, and we were out of there like rats off a sinking ship.

We were already in the street when he opened the café door behind us. "It is not so nice there, you know. There is much crime in that part of the city, near Le Bec Zinc."

"Thanks, Pierre," Mackenzie said with a wave as we practically ran up the street.

"I don't want you to think all French men are as vain as Pierre," Juliette said. "It was very sad to hear how he believed all your flattery."

"No sweat," Mac said. "We've got a lot of guys like him in New York, too—especially at Westside School. They've got, like, Tommy Hilfiger of the brain. It takes a while, but eventually most of them wise up to the fact that it's only a matter of eighteen inches between a pat on the back and a kick in the pants."

Juliette laughed and tapped the pavement loudly with her cane. I burst into laughter with her, as Mac took her arm and we headed up the hill and into a maze of dark, narrowing streets.

6

Maurice Cardin

Le Bec Zinc was a truly cheapo establishment, fitting right into its tacky neighborhood, with seedy shops and run-down markets. This was a far cry from the chic Riviera that glittered only half a mile away. The pension had a neon sign out front that was only half working. We climbed the chipped stone steps and pounded on the front door.

It didn't open, but a window on our left did, and out popped the upper half of a large, middle-aged woman with missing front teeth and a suspicious squint. She barked a question at us in French, and Juliette answered politely. The lady said something else, retreated back inside, and slammed the window shut.

"What was that all about?" Mackenzie asked.

"She is the concierge, " Juliette explained. "She takes care of the hotel. She said to wait, please."

The door creaked open. It was old, and oak, and must have weighed half a ton. We were faced with the formidable lady once more. This time, she spoke to us in English, barely understandable. "So, you are Americans?"

She looked Mackenzie and me up and down like we were freaks.

"Yes, ma'am," I said. "We're searching for someone who may have stayed here at your hotel."

"Mmm," she said, frowning. "And why should I help you find him?"

I shot Mackenzie a look and reached out to touch Juliette's arm, warning her to keep silent. "He stole money from our friend Juliette here, and we came to get it back. Naturally, there would be a reward for you if we found him."

The concierge looked at Juliette, her face softening a bit. "Reward, eh? Okay. *Entrez*."

We followed her to a couple of threadbare sofas in the front room and sat down. Mackenzie described the man Pierre had seen, long, dark hair, baseball cap, expensive designer clothing, carrying a wad of large bills (*Juliette's* money, we added), and gave her the date in question. "Ah, *oui*," she said, making a face. "Maurice Cardin."

"Maurice Cardin?" I repeated.

"Is he still here?" Juliette asked.

"No, he leave after one or two nights. He always sneak in and out. I never see his face too well. But I remember his voice. He speak like a show-off. *Pugh!*" She made a spitting sound and waved her hand dismissively.

"What do you mean, *show-off*?" Mackenzie asked.

"He butcher *le français*. He speak fast, and he squash

44

his words like *les Parisiens*. And he have a strange accent," she added. "I think perhaps South African or Australian—or maybe American, like you. Also, he pay in five-hundred-franc notes. Something I do not see every day."

"Is there anything else?" I asked. "Anything that might help us find him?"

Madame snorted. "He leave his shirt. I keep it for a week from the kindness of my heart. But he never return, so I discard it."

We followed her outside, where she fished the shirt out of the trash.

"Madame," Juliette said. "Could I please have this shirt? Perhaps it will help us find him."

"Take it. Why should I care? I think you will reward me for that, too, no?"

The concierge stared at me expectantly.

Suddenly, Juliette began to cry. "Oh, P.C., we will never find my money!" She sobbed, lunging at me. I hugged her and attempted a few lame grunts of comfort. Mackenzie stood there with her mouth open.

"*Grandmère* will never recover from this. She trust me with that money and now it is lost!" She let go of me and collapsed to the ground. Man, this girl was talented.

"Ah, forget it," the woman said, looking at Juliette as though she'd like to throw *her* in the trash. "I cannot take this sobbing. Just go." With that, she turned and shuffled back inside.

So we left. Fast.

Mackenzie laughed as we rounded the nearest corner. "That was amazing, Juliette!"

"Bravo!" I added, clapping.

Juliette curtsied. "*Merci beaucoup*. I keep the shirt because of the scent," Juliette said, her face glowing with excitement. "It clings to the shirt for a long time. Tomorrow we bring it to the police station, and give it to the lab. The chemist there is trained to smell like a bloodhound. He will know the aftershave or deodorant on this shirt, I am sure of it. And I am sure that he will confirm my suspicion. I have an excellent nose, P.C. and Mackenzie. It is an American scent, I am sure."

From an American killer? I wondered as we entered the train station, heading back to Monaco and our hotel.

7

Will the Real Grim Shady Please Stand Up?

It was late by the time we left the train station in Monaco. We were all hungry, but we decided to make a quick stop at the police station to drop off Maurice Cardin's shirt. It was the latest piece of evidence in the case, and one that we hoped would nail Cyrano.

Inspector LeSeur greeted us with a big smile. "Ah, how is it with my little deputy and her friends?" he asked.

Juliette told him, in French, about our day's adventure in Nice. LeSeur seemed impressed. "*Eh bien*, you did better than the police! Many thanks to you."

"Juliette says it's an American scent on the shirt," I told LeSeur.

"Yes. We will test, of course, but already I believe her. My daughter's nose, it is *formidable*. But for now, you must all rest from your labor. Here, we have a suspect under arrest already."

"A suspect? *Who?*" Mackenzie asked.

"Monsieur Tomas Milano," LeSeur said. "We caught him trying to sell Dr. Epstein-Hopper's Cartier watch at a pawnshop on avenue de la Costa."

"Whoa!" I said. "So *he's* Cyrano?"

LeSeur made a face. "I do not know. He has an alibi for the morning Dr. Epstein-Hopper was killed, and his girlfriend made bail for him. So now we must let him go. Anyway," he continued, "there is no guarantee that he is truly the Cyrano killer, even if he has to do with this murder."

"You're going to set him free?" Mackenzie repeated, dumbstruck.

"For the moment, we have no choice," LeSeur said with a shrug.

Juliette had to stay with her dad, so Mackenzie and I arranged to meet her for breakfast at our hotel the next morning. The two of us headed outside, on our way back to the hotel. Just as we reached the bottom of the stone steps, we heard a commotion behind us. Tomas Milano had emerged from the station, surrounded by LeSeur and three other police officers, and was being freed from handcuffs. He sneered at LeSeur and said, "*Ciao, Ispettore.* You will be sorry you have inconvenienced me. My lawyer will be calling you soon."

He came down the steps and rushed past without even seeing the two of us. With a quick nod between us, Mackenzie and I started trailing Milano, keeping a safe distance behind. He was walking at a pretty fast clip, and the streets were crowded, so it was hard to keep him in sight. Finally, though, we saw him disappear into a club whose neon sign read LE BOOM-BOOM ROOM.

"Now what?" Mackenzie asked. "Do we really want to go in there?"

"Great. So what do we do? Just wait here for him to come back out?"

"I don't know about you, but I'm starving. And the food at the hotel was pretty incredible last night. I say we call it a day and go stuff our faces."

"Sounds good," I said. "I don't think too well when I'm hungry anyway."

We returned to the hotel just in time for the late dinner seating. We heaped our plates high at the hotel's buffet—everything from roast lamb to beef bourguignon and lyonnaise potatoes—and sat down at a table near a huge ice sculpture of a pheasant to eat and think.

"So, let's see," I started. "How many suspects have we got?"

"Well, there's Dr. Hopper," Mackenzie said. "He's suspect A. He was the victim's husband, after all, and we already know he was cavorting behind his wife's back with Dr. White."

"That would make her suspect B," I added. "And of course, there's that sleazy Tomas who thinks he's God's gift to lonely women."

"Suspect C. And don't forget Maurice Cardin, whoever he is. We know he's at least connected to Genevieve Blanc's killing," Mackenzie said, between bites of her rare filet mignon with béarnaise sauce and scalloped squash.

"Right. I doubt Dr. Hopper or Dr. White could be Cyrano, though. I mean he's been killing women in France for two years. I suppose it could be Milano."

"I say we check out our three main suspects some more," Mackenzie said. "And try to find out more about this mystery Cardin who smells like an American!"

"Tomorrow for that," I said. "I don't know about you, but I've gotta get some shut-eye."

I didn't sleep well at all. I kept dreaming of Juliette being stalked by a maniac with a cleaver. I was incredibly relieved the next morning when Dr. Riggs woke us up to tell us that Juliette was waiting for us in the lobby.

She was practically jumping up and down by the time we got dressed and down there. "I have much news to tell you!"

"Come on, let's get some breakfast," Mackenzie said. "Neither of us can think until we've got some food in our stomachs."

"Okay, so what's the news?" I asked as we sat down to our international breakfasts: eggs Benedict for me; eggs Florentine for Mackenzie; Juliette opted for Belgian waffles with a side of crisp bacon.

"My papa has been very busy," Juliette said. "He says Dr. Hopper's alibi is confirmed by the people at the Café Corniche where he have his breakfast. They say he come there around seven A.M. yesterday, and he ask them so many questions about Monaco that they cannot forget him. So now, with this and the hotel surveillance tapes, my papa says he could not have killed his wife."

"Hmm," I said, tapping my fork on my plate. "That does sound pretty airtight. But I don't know about Milano's alibi. His girlfriend could be lying. I say we go talk to her today."

"She is—how you call it?—an exotic dancer. My papa say she works at a club here in Monte Carlo."

"Le Boom-Boom Room!" Mackenzie said.

Juliette nodded. "But about Cyrano, there is also news. Papa say the tuberose clue has led the police to several suspects, four men and one woman."

"Here? In Monaco?" I asked, surprised.

"*Mais non*. In Paris," Juliette answered. "In Monaco, they have found nothing so far. Only the shirt we gave Papa."

"But," I said, "if he or she is one of the ones in Paris, that would mean whoever killed Dr. Epstein-Hopper, and probably Genevieve Blanc, wasn't Cyrano at all. We'd have a copycat killer on our hands."

"Copycat?" Juliette repeated, looking confused.

"It means someone who wanted to imitate Cyrano," I explained.

"So it looks like we ought to concentrate on our potential copycats, then," Mackenzie said.

"Right," I said. "Maurice Cardin, from what we heard, never let himself be seen in good lighting, always left and returned to the pension when the concierge would not see him, and wore a hat down low over his face."

"Maurice Cardin did not want to be recognized," Juliette said. "He would have worn a disguise!"

"That's what I'm thinking, too," I said. "It would also explain why a guy who dresses well and obviously has a lot of money would stay in a cheapo pension. He'd want to preserve his anonymity. And," I continued as something else occurred to me, "there's no reason to think that the name itself wasn't fake, too."

"It's possible that one of the other three suspects could have been Maurice Cardin in disguise," Mackenzie added. "Even Dr. White could pass for a man, I'll bet. She looks a little mannish, and that voice of hers sounds like she plays tight end for the Pittsburgh Steelers."

"That would mean that Dr. White or Dr. Hopper would have been on the Côte d'Azur the week before," Juliette noted. "We could check on that."

"And, let's not forget that Maurice Cardin could be none of the other three," Mackenzie said. "He could still be the real Cyrano. Although it is odd that Genevieve Blanc and Dr. Epstein-Hopper were the only Cyrano victims outside Paris. It does suggest a copycat."

"I don't think Le Boom-Boom Room will be open this early," Juliette said.

"Probably not," I agreed. "But we can start today with

Dr. White. She's giving her speech this morning."

So that was what we did. Dr. White's speech was a long one, all about serial killers, their psychology, and profiling. A lot of it we'd already seen by reading her computer notes. When she was done speaking, a large group of colleagues wanted to chat with her. We'd missed our chance.

Finally, after lunch, we cornered her as she entered the elevator to ride back up to her suite. "Dr. White?" I began. "I really admired your speech this morning."

"Did you now?" she asked, seeming pleased with herself.

"So did I!" Mackenzie joined in.

"*Et moi aussi!* Me, too!" Juliette added.

Dr. White smiled. "Yes, it did seem to go over rather well."

The elevator opened at her floor, and we got off with her, walking with her as she headed down the hallway toward her suite. I immediately noticed a distinct weave in her walk, which indicated that she'd had a few too many Chardonnays with lunch.

Perfect, I thought. It was now or never. "I had never heard of that Myra Hindley case and those murders on the Hattersley moors in England," I said. "It was really an eye-opener to hear how she helped knock off twelve guys with an ax and then liked to have her photo taken standing at their fresh graves in her backyard. So many people showed up to hear you."

"Having Dr. Epstein-Hopper 'knocked off' helped my attendance, I'm sure," Dr. White said, fishing in her purse for her key card.

"I understand you and Harriet Epstein-Hopper went to graduate school together," Mackenzie said, as Dr. White opened the door.

"And what fun that was," Dr. White replied. Then, seeing us still standing there, she added, "Well, good-bye. And thanks for the kind words."

"Wow," Mackenzie said, ignoring her and boldly crossing the suite's threshold, "your digs are really high up! So much better than the ones they gave you at first." She went straight to the window to admire the view.

Dr. White went after her as if she were going to grab her by the scruff of her neck. Seizing the moment when her back was turned to us, I took Juliette's arm and ushered her inside. "You know, Dr. White," I said, "I've been worrying about Cyrano since we first spoke to you. Juliette here seems to fit the profile. We wouldn't want anything to happen to her."

Dr. White halted at the suite bar and poured herself another glass of wine. "No, we wouldn't want that, now would we? I'll be right back," she muttered as she disappeared into the bedroom.

She reentered a moment later, still wearing the white shirt and man's tie she'd had on before. This time, though, the shirt was untucked—she had changed into different, more casual pants. Mackenzie and I exchanged a knowing look. Apparently men weren't the only ones wearing those hot new Massimo pants.

"Can you tell us more about Dr. Epstein-Hopper?" Mackenzie asked. "We're trying to understand the type of victims Cyrano goes after."

"Harriet? Ha—we went way back," Dr. White collapsed onto the sofa with her glass still in her hand. Her eyes were half shut, and she seemed lost in the past. "Here's to you, girl. Can't say I'll miss you. But I'm sorry you had to go *that* way."

"Sounds as if you didn't like her," I said, stating the obvious.

"She hated me as much as I hated her," Dr. White said. She had a slight smile on her face, but her tone was bitter. "We've been enemies since our grad school days at Columbia. Even then, she was always a pain. So competitive! Nobody wanted her in their lab group, because she'd hog all the credit for whatever you did."

She downed her wine, then got up and poured herself another. "Don't mind me," she told us. "I'm celebrating. My speech this morning got me five new speaking engagements and a book offer! It's amazing what you can accomplish when your chief obstacle gets herself killed."

"Your chief obstacle?" Juliette echoed.

"That was Harriet," she said, raising her glass in another toast to the dead woman. "Always beating me out for awards and men! It didn't matter that I was twice as brilliant, younger, and better-looking. She was twice as pushy, and that's what counts in this world."

"She stole men from you, too?" Mackenzie prompted.

"She'd throw an egg into an electric fan if it'd get her attention," Dr. White remembered with a sneer. "Dyed her hair red at Bergdorf's just recently. She used to be dirty blond, and before that, gray. Ha! Not that it helped her keep Richard interested."

"Are you suggesting there were problems in their marriage?" I asked, since Dr. White seemed well past the point of being discreet.

"Problems? Ha!" she brayed. "He couldn't stand it either that she was more successful than he was! Who could live with her, though? You've gotta feel sorry for Richard, pathetic as he is. I'm glad he didn't kill her, but don't you believe for one minute that he's all broken up about it. It's as liberating for him as it is for me."

She froze, then looked up, seeming to notice us for the first time. "Oh, God. I don't feel very well suddenly. Please leave me alone." She got up and stumbled back into the suite's bathroom.

We looked at each other. "That was interesting," said Mackenzie. "And those were some pretty nice pants, huh?"

"Sure were," I agreed. "Let's go."

We left Dr. White's room and headed back downstairs in the elevator. "Boy, is she ever a loose cannon!" Mac said.

"Yeah, but do you think she killed Dr. Epstein-Hopper?" I wondered out loud.

"She really hated her," Juliette pointed out. "And she was able to do it. She had the suite next door. And there are no cameras inside the suites to catch her."

"The victim would have had to open the connecting door to let her in," I reminded Juliette.

"Maybe she *did*," Mackenzie said. "They knew each other, after all. But what about this: if Dr. White and Dr. Hopper were in it together, he could have unlocked his side of the door before he left to go jogging. That would give him an airtight alibi, and he'd still be guilty!"

"I don't know," I said. "If they're in it together, she did a pretty poor job of covering her tracks just now. Sure, she's pretty twisted. But she's not acting very guilty. And *if* they were in it together, wouldn't they have thought up an alibi for her, too?"

"Besides," Mackenzie added, "why would she and Dr. Hopper kill this Genevieve Blanc person?"

It was a good question, one of many we didn't have the answers for. At least, not yet.

8

Two-Armed Bandit

We caught up with Dr. Richard Hopper talking to Mackenzie's dad outside the dining room, where the luncheon for convention participants had just ended. "I'm going to have Harriet buried at sea," he was saying. "Just as soon as the police release her body to me. She would have liked that, I know. She had once even mentioned how she might have liked us to retire on the French Riviera. She just loved the Mediterranean."

Dr. Riggs nodded. "We'll all be with you in spirit when you do, Richard," he said. "But if you'd like some company, I'd be happy to come along with you. Harriet was a brilliant and generous colleague and friend."

"Oh, no! I mean—ah—no, that won't be necessary, Dolan. Thank you, though. I appreciate the thought."

"You're sure?"

"Positive. Harriet wouldn't have wanted a fuss made over her. Besides, I want it to be a . . . private moment. You understand."

"Of course," Dr. Riggs said, clasping him on the arm. "You're holding up well, Richard. I'm proud of you."

"Thank you," Dr. Hopper said hoarsely. Then he looked up, and noticed us. "Ah, hello there," he said.

"Richard, this is my daughter, Mackenzie, and her friends, P.C. and Juliette," Dr. Riggs said, smiling. "They're quite the young detectives."

Dr. Hopper looked at us as if he didn't know whether to laugh or cry.

"Yes, they've solved quite a few cases," Dr. Riggs went on. "And now they seem to be sniffing around this Cyrano fellow. I've warned them to stay away from it, and I hope they've been paying attention." This last was sent our way with a meaningful look combined with a hesitancy, as if he'd caught himself with his foot in his mouth. Discretion was never one of his strong cards.

"We were just on our way to the beach for the afternoon," Mackenzie assured her dad and Dr. Hopper. "Weren't we, guys?"

"Oh, yes!" Juliette said.

"Uh-huh," I confirmed.

"Good," Dr. Riggs said. "Well, I've got to run. Hang in there, Richard. Enjoy the beach, kids!" He left us with a smile and an awkward wave.

Dr. Hopper hadn't finished looking us over. "So you're interested in Cyrano?" he asked, his voice shaky.

"Sort of," Mackenzie hedged.

I knew what she was thinking. We hadn't really had a chance to plan our line of attack, and now he'd caught us off guard. I had a trial balloon, however, that was inflating in the back of my mind. I wanted to test it out on Hopper. "Actually," I said, "we're wondering if your wife's killer wasn't a *copycat*."

Hopper raised his eyebrows in surprise. "Really? The police seem to think it was Cyrano. What makes you think it wasn't?"

I wasn't going to tell him about the tuberose or the shirt with the "American scent," but I did want to set off alarm bells. If he was our man, what I was about to say would throw him into a panic.

"All Cyrano's previous crimes took place in Paris, and his victims had long red hair," I said. "Only the past two crimes were different. They took place on the Riviera, and the victims had medium-length red hair. We think Cyrano is a careful, fastidious, methodical killer. That's why he hasn't been caught. A person like that doesn't suddenly change a winning strategy."

I'd never put it all together like that before, but I thought my analysis was right on target. Mackenzie and Juliette nodded their agreement.

Dr. Hopper snorted. "You're quite mistaken," he said. "A really clever serial killer changes his modus operandi every so often, precisely to avoid becoming predictable. Don't take my word for it. Ask Dr. Francine White. She's the serial-killer expert."

Mac gave him a look of intense gratitude. "We'll be sure to do that."

"I'll give you kids one other piece of advice," Dr.

Hopper said, locking his gaze onto me. "Keep your noses out of my wife's death. For God's sake, the poor woman has suffered enough. Let her rest in peace." He turned on his heels and strode away.

"Yikes," Mackenzie said under her breath. "Somebody doesn't want us investigating this thing."

"*Nobody* does, Mac," I pointed out. "Haven't you noticed?"

The hotel concierge told us that Le Boom-Boom Room didn't open till eight P.M., so we decided to keep our promise to Mac's dad and go down to the beach. Juliette went to check in with her dad at the police station. In spite of the fact that we had only two more days before we left for home, Mac and I needed to decompress, to think, and take a little breather.

Before we went to catch some rays, I picked up the phone in our suite and put in a call to Jesus. That's Jesus Lopez of Manhattan, a freshman now at Westside School, and one of our good buddies. In fact, Jesus is our computer guru. Whenever we need some research done on a case, he's our guy.

"Yo, it's us! We're in Monaco, dude," I said when he answered. "Yeah, wish you were here, too!"

He caught us up on some news from home, and when he'd finished, Mackenzie, on the other extension, filled him in on our Cyrano case.

"We need some help," I told him.

"You name it, bro'."

"Could you check out Dr. Hopper's routine at the New York Athletic Club? How often he goes, stuff like that?"

"Sure thing," Jesus said.

"Also, check with the salon at Bergdorf's about Harriet Epstein-Hopper's dye job," Mackenzie said. "And maybe ask their condo doormen about any goings-on between Dr. Hopper and Dr. White. You know, anything they might have seen or overheard."

"You got it," Jesus assured us.

"One more thing," I added. "Any criminal records on one Tomas Milano, working on the French Riviera, Paris, Monaco—even Italy. Oh, and check to see if you can find anything on this Maurice Cardin."

"Gimme . . . oh, let's say . . . four hours," Jesus said.

"Outstanding!" Mackenzie said. "I'll have my cell phone on."

We had an early dinner, and afterward, headed straight over to Le Boom-Boom Room. We figured Milano's girlfriend would be getting there as early as seven o'clock. We wanted to catch her before she went in. We had Juliette meet us there.

"My papa gave me the girlfriend's name," Juliette told us. "Nicole DuBois. She is tall, like me, with a green streak in her long platinum hair."

We were in luck. At that very moment, we saw a

woman matching Juliette's description headed in our direction. She looked like that blond avenger in those old Clint Eastwood movies.

"Mademoiselle DuBois?" I said, stepping forward as she reached us by the club's front door.

"*Oui*," she said, looking us over suspiciously. "What you want?"

"We'd like to talk to you," Mackenzie said.

"About Tomas," Juliette added. "And about the Cyrano killer."

Nicole DuBois glared at us. "You little brats!" she hissed. "Do not speak to me of this! My Tomas, he is no angel, but he is no killer either! Go play on the beach rock, you nosy little rodents. Mind your own business! Leave me and Tomas alone!" She wheeled around and pushed open the club's front door. A moment later, she was gone.

"Well, that wasn't too cool," Mackenzie commented.

"Not at all," I concurred. "Man, I'll bet you she's calling Tomas right now to warn him about us."

Mackenzie gave me a troubled look. "You think?"

"This is terrific," I said. "Every one of our suspects, with the possible exception of Maurice Cardin, now knows we're on their tail. Whoever's guilty might start considering desperate measures. I mean, this is someone who's killed before."

"You've got a point there," she agreed.

"Still, we must go on," Juliette insisted. "We must

stop the killer somehow, before he or she strikes again."

Mackenzie and I knew she was right, and that we wouldn't quit until it was over. Or at least until we had to fly back to the States.

We headed back to the Monte Carlo Grand Hotel, and entered via the casino entrance, because it was nearest. Coming in this way, we had to cross the huge gaming floor to get to the hotel wings of the building. Because we were underage, we had to stay on the central red carpet that split the gaming floor in two, the only legal path for minors through the casino.

There was a cacophony of noise: bells ringing, sirens wailing, coins jangling, and the thump-thump of the one-armed bandits being pulled again and again and again. People stood by the machines, their faces frozen in rapt attention, feeding more and more coins into the slots. Not one of them was smiling, I noticed. As soon as they won a few coins, they dropped them back into the slot and kept pulling that arm. The whole landscape was surreal and disorienting, like a freakazoid nightmare.

Just as we were passing a bandstand where a local lounge group was singing a loud cover of "Funky Town," Mackenzie's cell phone went off.

"Hello?" she yelled into it. "I can't hear you. Jesus?"

I guided Mackenzie past the lounge act amplifiers to a cul-de-sac near the one-hundred-franc slots. It was a little quieter, and with my head next to hers, I could hear some of what Jesus was telling her.

"What have you got?" Mac asked.

"Not much," Jesus said. After that, I only made out a word or two over the static and din of the casino. I had to wait for her to hang up before I got the full lowdown.

"He says the only weird thing he's come across so far is that it was Dr. Hopper who got his wife to dye her hair red. He made her appointment at Bergdorf's salon himself."

"That's planning ahead if I ever heard it," I said. "I mean, if you're plotting to whack your wife Cyrano-style."

"Totally," she said, nodding. "Jesus says he's still checking out the other stuff, but he wanted to let us know about the dye job right away."

"Good thinking." And then it hit me. "Hey, where's *Juliette*?"

"Omigod!" Mackenzie gasped, spinning around. "Juliette! Where are you?" she cried out. We both shouted, but our voices were lost in the casino clamor. And so was Juliette.

"Where could she have gone?" I wondered. "And why would she have kept going without us?"

"She wouldn't have," Mackenzie answered. "Unless . . ."

"Unless what?" I muttered, but I already knew the answer, and I didn't like it one bit!

The Unexpected

We began to backtrack and comb the casino aisles, although the staff kept shouting at us to get back on the central red-carpet strip. We figured out that Juliette wouldn't have been allowed off it either. We spotted a staff area between the gaming tables and the hotel lobby. It was a dimly lit, curving passageway that was lined with bank machines, rest rooms, and rows of house phones. We ran yelling into the rest rooms, with no success.

Mackenzie cried out that she felt a sense of dread that made her scalp tingle—always a bad sign.

Suddenly, we heard what sounded like a whimpering coming from behind the door of a utility closet. I pounded on the door, calling "Juliette! Let us in!"

There was a scream from inside, followed by a muffled sound, as if a hand had been clapped over her mouth. "Security!" I yelled, and Mac ran off to call for some muscle.

From behind the door, I heard the sounds of scuffling, and a man's muttering voice. Just as Mackenzie returned, with a pair of burly security guards in tow, the closet door burst open, and Tomas Milano emerged, brandishing a knife big enough to decapitate a bull.

He pointed it at me, then at Mackenzie and the guards, before running down the hallway toward the casino exit. The two guards ran after him, leaving me and Mac to take care of Juliette.

She was alive, unhurt, but shaken. "He dragged me into the closet!" she said, trying to choke back sobs. "He put the knife to my neck, and he tell me to keep quiet. Then he tell me to stay out . . ."

"Stay out of what?" I asked.

"The murder. He said for us to keep away from him and Nicole, or he will kill us all!"

The security men returned. "He got away," a short fat one said. "Ran through the bar and into the kitchen. We almost had him, but he threw down a rack of pots and pans. We couldn't get to him."

"Don't worry," the other one said. "We have alerted the police. They will be here soon, and they will make sure he is caught."

Sure enough, Juliette's dad arrived shortly afterward, with a contingent of local police. "From now on," he told us, "you three will go nowhere without protection. And Juliette," he turned to her with a stern gaze, "you will stay close to me, *tu comprends?*"

"*Oui, Papa,*" Juliette said in a small, scared voice.

"This Milano, he will not stay at large for long,"

Inspector LeSeur said. "Perhaps he will flee to France, or to Italy, but no matter. We will catch up to him soon." He turned to his officers. "Perhaps he is our Cyrano killer. For sure, he has threatened violence against these young people, and for that, he will be stopped."

For a while, our investigation slowed to a grinding halt. We were in the constant company of two uniformed policemen who followed us everywhere we went (except inside our suite, in which case they politely waited outside, guarding the doors).

Since it was late, and Juliette was still freaked out by her close encounter with Tomas Milano and his big knife, we called it a night, and arranged to meet in our suite the next morning.

Juliette came by around seven A.M., just as Dr. Riggs was going downstairs to attend a breakfast meeting. We gathered on the suite's terrace, ordered room service, and stared out at the yachts anchored offshore and in the nearby marina. It was the start of another glorious day, our fourth here in Monaco, and Mackenzie's and my last full day before returning to the U.S. The psychoanalyst conference would be winding up the following morning, and we were scheduled to take an early evening flight back to the States.

As we nibbled on our croissants and sipped our cappuccinos, we tried to make sense of what had happened so far, and add up the facts we'd unearthed, to see if we could get a glimpse of the big picture.

"So, is *Tomas* the real Cyrano?" Mackenzie began.

"It begins to look as if he at least killed Genevieve Blanc and Dr. Epstein-Hopper," Juliette said. "If not, why would he put the knife to my throat?"

"I don't know," I said. "If he was the killer, why didn't he just finish you off when he had the chance? Maybe he was just trying to send us a message. I mean, he had a good racket going down here before we started nosing into things. Now the police are all over him, and he can't make a living scamming rich old ladies anymore. That alone could have made him angry enough to threaten you, Juliette."

"But he say to stop looking into the murders!" she protested.

I thought about it for a moment. "True, but I don't think he's Cyrano, even though I don't think the Paris serial killer committed the last two murders either. He's always been too much of a perfectionist. Too ritualistic to vary his routine."

"*Non*, it is not likely either of the Paris suspects," Juliette agreed. "If one of them is Cyrano, he would have had to make a quick trip down here, then go right back to Paris."

"That's a big if," Mac said.

"What about our four Riviera suspects?" I asked. "Dr. Hopper, Dr. White, Milano, and Maurice Cardin?"

"If it is Milano," Juliette said, "he is on the run now. Soon the police will catch him."

"What about Dr. Hopper and Dr. White?" I asked. "If it's one of them, or the two of them as a team, wouldn't their passports show that they were in France last week, at the time of Genevieve Blanc's murder?"

Mackenzie quickly saw the hole in my intriguing new thought. "Not necessarily, P.C. Fake passports are easily bought and sold, especially by rich Americans. Besides, why would any American murder Genevieve Blanc? What's the connection?"

The idea still gnawed at me. "Something is missing," I said. "It is right in front of us, but we don't see it."

"So what's our next move?" Mackenzie asked. "We're kind of limited with those policemen following us everywhere we go."

"There's one place we could go and still do some productive work," I said.

"Where's that?" Mackenzie wondered.

"The police station. Remember, we still haven't played the hotel's videotapes ourselves. By now, they'll probably let us have a look at them."

Half an hour later, we were parked on steel folding chairs in front of a monitor, going over six hours' worth of videotape of the outside of the Hoppers' suite. It was a demonically painful way to kill our last day on the Riviera, but there didn't seem to be any better avenue of investigation open to us. Sitting and watching footage of a mostly empty hallway can really get to you, especially since we didn't want to fast-forward and chance missing something important, so after a while we all got pretty punchy. Mac started making up limericks about Cyrano, and drove us crazy with those for a good hour. At lunchtime we ordered ham-and-brie sandwiches, which we ate in front of the tube. Unfortunately, Juliette had caught the limerick bug, too, so they both tortured me with silly poems for the remainder of our time there. When the six hours were finally over, we were as clueless as the police had been. There was nothing there. Nothing at all. And yet . . .

I couldn't put my finger on it, or say why, but something was bothering me. I asked Mackenzie whether she felt the same way, and she said her scalp was tingling all over the place. Of course, Juliette could only know what we described seeing, but we began to wonder if we shouldn't look at the tapes all over again.

But just then, there was a commotion in the hallway outside our viewing room. People were shouting in French, sounding happy and triumphant. Juliette jumped up, her large and sightless blue eyes aglow with excitement.

"What?" I asked her. "What is it?"

"They catch him!" she cried exultantly. "They arrest Cyrano!"

10

Van Gogh Was Framed

We soon had all the details of the man they captured. Cyrano had not been one of the Paris suspects. In fact, he'd been found in Dijon, a city about midway between Paris and Nice–Monaco (which suggested that he could have reached either place with equal ease). And he was not one of our local suspects, either. Of course, he could have used the disguise of Maurice Cardin, but he was neither Tomas Milano, Dr. Richard Hopper, nor Dr. Francine White.

I cannot tell you the bizarre sense of mixed relief and disappointment both Mackenzie and I felt at this news. On the one hand, it was terrific that Cyrano was in custody. He'd been found with candles and photos of his victims, and had already confessed to several of the murders. This meant that redheaded women all over France could breathe easier, including Juliette and her mother.

On the other hand, Mac and I had had nothing whatsoever to do with his capture. All the running around we'd been doing, it seemed, had been for nothing, unless you counted the total exposure of Tomas Milano and his rich-old-lady racket. The cops could lock him up for a while and stop his scam in Monaco.

Juliette, on the other hand, was totally elated. It had been her tuberose clue that had led directly to the capture of Louis Verdun, alias Cyrano, a thirty-two-year-old loner who worked as an accountant by day and stalked women by night. He was turning out to be a character who totally fit Dr. White's profile of a serial killer.

The police found Verdun's apartment decorated with playbills from various productions of Edmund Rostand's classic play, *Cyrano de Bergerac*, and festooned with red roses, both living and dead. There were framed obituaries and newspaper accounts of the deaths of some of his victims hanging on the walls. Polaroids of each of the murdered girls in her final resting pose were tacked to the headboard of his bed. And there was cologne containing tuberose in his medicine cabinet.

"Juliette, you will come with me at once to Dijon," Inspector LeSeur told his daughter.

"*Oui, Papa,*" she said calmly, but I could tell she was psyched to go. As Mac and I both knew, Juliette had been obsessed with the Cyrano case far longer than either of us. It was only right she be there at the end, with her dad.

We said *au revoir* to Juliette—not good-bye, but "see you again." We hoped it was true. She promised to call and e-mail to fill us in on everything as more details came out. She kissed us on both cheeks, and then she was off to pack.

The inspector lingered with Mac and me. "I have some other news for you," he said. "It seems Tomas Milano was spotted at the border this morning, fleeing to Italy. The police protection for you is no longer necessary. I believe you can rest easy that Monsieur Milano will not be back in Monaco any time soon. The theft of Dr. Epstein-Hopper's Cartier watch, and his threats of violence against Juliette, have made him not just a petty criminal, but a felon. If he returns to Monaco, or even to France, he will be caught. In Italy, where he has friends and family, he can hide, perhaps. But only for a short while. In the end, his greed with lead him back to us."

Mackenzie and I left the police station in a daze, not sure what to do with ourselves. It was a lot to digest: Cyrano's capture, Milano's flight, Juliette's sudden departure. Only half an hour before, we had been busy investigating Dr. Epstein-Hopper's murder.

Now it felt like we had been on a roller-coaster, but in a weird way we wanted to get right back on in the front seat. We missed the investigation. We missed something. . . .

We returned to the Monte Carlo Grand Hotel, and went up to our suite to try to snap out of our funk. Dr. Riggs was there, relaxing on the terrace, reading the

International Herald Tribune to catch up on the news from back home. "Hi, there," he greeted us. "How's it going? Still got your police escorts?"

"Nope," Mackenzie said, depressed.

We caught her dad up on current events, and his smile told us he was relieved at the news. "Well, now," he said. "Sounds like you two ought to use the rest of your time here to sightsee and kick back. Have you been to the Oceanographic Institute yet?"

"Not yet, Daddy," Mackenzie confessed. "I really am interested, but it's a little late to go today. We'll check it out early tomorrow morning and be back in time to leave for the airport."

"Do that," he said, nodding contentedly. "By the way, tonight there's a gala dinner cruise on the Mediterranean for us headshrinkers and our guests. That means you two are invited. How about it?"

I wondered if Dr. Hopper and Dr. White would be aboard. Probably. It wouldn't be a bad idea for us to go along, just to keep an eye on them. "What time does it start?" I asked.

"We gather at the dock at seven P.M. and depart at seven-thirty. So be there or be square," Dr. Riggs quipped.

"Okay, Daddy," Mackenzie said, and gave him a kiss.

He gave her a quick hug and then waved us off. "Meanwhile, go and enjoy yourselves. You deserve a break."

And so we did. Well, not really. We spent another hour on the beach, but we couldn't get our minds off the case. Was it really over? Had the police in Dijon arrested the man who was not only Cyrano, but also the killer of Genevieve Blanc and Dr. Harriet Epstein-Hopper? Had a ritualistic killer, a man of fastidious habits, really altered his routine just to throw off the police?

Or were we about to let a copycat killer escape our grasp? If we left Monaco the next day without finding out, a vicious, sick killer might go scot-free. It seemed that the police were all too happy to pin the last two killings on Cyrano and be done with it.

The phone rang a little after seven o'clock, just as we were getting dressed up and ready to race down to the dock.

"Hello?" Mac said, flipping open the mouthpiece. Then, "Hey, Juliette! Whoa . . . really! . . . no, black . . . uh-huh . . . definitely . . . okay, do that, yeah . . . bye."

"Hey!" I complained. "What was that all about?"

"It was Juliette," Mac said, looking as though the windmills of her mind were spinning like crazy.

"You hung up without even letting me talk to her!" I griped.

"She was in a hurry. She and her dad are flying back down here tonight! There's been an interesting turn in the case."

"What's that?" I asked.

"Cyrano confessed to all the seventeen killings in

Paris. He was proud of them, in fact. But he totally denied having anything to do with either of the murders down here. In fact, he acted offended when the police even suggested he was behind them."

"That's okay," I said. "But he could be lying. There's got to be more."

"There is," Mac said. "Juliette says all of Cyrano's e-mail messages had been in red, not black, like the one on Harriet's computer."

"So he could have slipped up."

"No way. Juliette said the guy's really a perfectionist freak," Mac said. I noticed her hands beginning to tremble. "Cyrano confessed that he was thinking of changing, that he had been planning one day soon to take souvenirs from a victim. He said he had written down the recipe and all, that he wanted to make a stew with onions and carrots and fingers." I saw her fight the fear that was growing inside of her. "He said the killer down here was 'tartuffish.' A faker. Like the character Tartuffe in the famous Molière play. Juliette says he talks about everything like it's show business. She said Cyrano used another word to describe him, too."

"Let me guess. Copycat," I said.

"Bingo," Mac said. "And the police think he's telling the truth. That's why Juliette and her dad are rushing back to Monaco. She called from the airport. They've got a special police plane."

I can't explain the rush of chills that shot through me

at that moment. All of a sudden, I was certain we were back in business. There was a case for us to solve, and not much time in which to do it."

"What do you think the police will do about it?" Mackenzie asked.

"Wrong question, Mac," I said. "The real question is, what are *we* going to do about it?"

11

Murder à la Mode

We raced down to the dock, only to see the dinner cruise boat pulling out into the harbor. "Jeez!" I growled, kicking at a railing. "There goes our chance to really grill our suspects again." We stood frozen in place for a few minutes. I was trying to think so hard my hair hurt.

"Oh, well," Mackenzie finally said. "Maybe there's something else we can accomplish in the meantime."

"How about we grab some dinner?" I suggested. My brain doesn't work too well without some protein, but I wasn't interested in catching any mad-cow ailments either. I felt like some good fish.

We jogged across the Place du Casino to a little café we'd noticed on avenue de la Madonne: Le Bon Appétit. We sat down at a sidewalk table, and ordered some mussels and a hot duck salad.

"What if Genevieve Blanc was killed by somebody else?" Mackenzie asked. "I mean, a different copycat altogether—let's say Maurice Cardin."

"Okay."

"And let's say Dr. White killed Harriet Epstein-Hopper—it makes the most sense, after all. She could have knocked on the door between their suites, and Harriet would have opened it, since they knew each other. Then she could have killed her, and made it look like a Cyrano killing."

"I follow you," I said. "But why would Maurice Cardin have tried to make Genevieve Blanc's murder look like Cyrano's work?"

"I don't know," she replied. "Maybe it was a coincidence. Maybe he was someone who knew her, and wanted to throw the police off his trail."

"It doesn't fit," I said. "If he knew Genevieve, then why would Maurice Cardin have checked into Le Bec Zinc, and taken the trouble to hide his identity there?"

"You got any better ideas?"

"I think I might," I said. A vague, foggy picture was beginning to form in my brain. "What if Genevieve and Harriet were killed by the same person, and that person was not Cyrano?"

"Yeah . . . ?"

"And what if—I know this sounds totally sicko—but what if Genevieve was killed *for practice*?"

"Practice? Oh my God! That is so twisted! That would mean the killer was just as sick and sadistic as Cyrano himself, and even more calculating."

"It's just a thought. But what if it's true? What if the real target all along was Harriet Epstein-Hopper, and the killer already had it in mind beforehand to make it look like the murderer was Cyrano? Wouldn't it be more convincing if he or she killed someone else down here as well? Someone with shorter red hair like Harriet's?"

"I see your point . . . I guess," Mackenzie said, not sounding totally convinced. "That would kind of eliminate Tomas Milano, though, wouldn't it?"

"Yeah," I agreed. "I can't see him going about things that way. First of all, he's never been known to kill strangers for their valuables, and odds are he didn't know Dr. Epstein-Hopper beforehand. Okay, let's look at the alternatives: Hopper and White. Hopper seems more obvious, because he's a guy, but I can't stop thinking about her Massimo pants and really masculine style. But, either way, if one of them *was* Maurice Cardin, they'd have had to get a false passport and arrive in France more than a week early."

"Why *more* than a week? Genevieve was killed only a week before Harriet."

"Because," I replied, "if it was one of those two, they'd have needed to scout around to find the perfect decoy victim—one who had Harriet's approximate hair length and color."

"So you don't think they'd have stayed at Le Bec Zinc that whole time, huh?"

"No," I said. "Too risky. The more time they spent there, the more likely they could be identified later.

More likely, they'd have stayed at some nicer place until they'd found their quarry. Then they'd have booked one or two nights at Le Bec Zinc, just before and after the crime. And after killing Genevieve, they'd have returned to their regular upscale digs."

"And where would those be?" Mackenzie asked.

I looked her right in the eye. "I'd be willing to take a wild guess." And then I turned to look at our hotel across the boulevard. "If he or she was scouting murders, what better place to stay than the place where they were planning to kill Harriet?"

"If Maurice Cardin stayed at the Monte Carlo Grand Hotel . . . then we could check the records and prove it!" she said. The old fire had crawled back into her eyes.

"Right! Let's go!" I turned to the startled waiter. "We'll be back in a few minutes," I promised, taking out a wad of francs and handing them over. "Just hold our food till we get back, okay?"

The waiter muttered something, but I knew I'd overpaid, so I didn't care. We ran back across the plaza and into the lavish lobby of the hotel. At the front desk we asked to see the last week's hotel register. The staff manager on duty eyed us like we were loonies from La Jolla. "To what purpose do you want to see such a thing?" he asked, sniffing. "It is highly irregular."

"It may have some bearing on the murder that happened here the other day," I explained.

"In that case, I suggest you call the police," he said, sticking out his chin.

Where was Juliette when we needed her? I sighed and handed the guy two hundred francs. "That won't be necessary, now, will it?" I asked.

He considered the bills on the desk for a moment, looking around for potential witnesses then grabbed them. He brought out a large, leather-bound book, and plopped it down on an empty desk. *"Voilà."*

We sat down and started flipping through the pages, while our new French friend looked over our shoulders.

"Look, P.C.!" Mackenzie gasped. "It's Maurice Cardin!"

Sure enough. There next to a signature that was really nothing more than a scribble was the name, printed on the register. Maurice Cardin had registered at the Monte Carlo Grand Hotel the night after Genevieve Blanc was murdered.

I flipped forward to the day we checked in and found Dr. White's handwriting. No match. Then we searched the register and saw Dr. Hopper's signature. Sure enough, it looked like Maurice Cardin's writing. I flipped back and ran my finger along the line to the right of Cardin's name, and there it was, suite 307. The same suite as the Hoppers'.

"Omigod," Mackenzie said.

"I think this will do as proof that Hopper's our guy," I said. "But I want to check one more thing." I turned back to the manager. "We need to see the videos of the second-floor hallway from the night Maurice Cardin checked in."

"That is impossible, without a direct order from the police," he said, as if I'd just asked him to shear his pet poodle in January.

I had a very strong hunch and I wasn't going to give up on it so easily. "Then at least see if you have the tapes," I insisted. "We'll have the police in here soon enough to get them."

The manager looked like he wanted to stab me with the desk pen, but he restrained himself. He gave us a little nod, and went off to the side and phoned the hotel security. We couldn't understand everything he said, but after a long while he returned to face us. He looked really flustered.

"I do not understand it. All tapes are conserved here on a shelf for one year before we discard them. But the tape for the morning about which you inquire, it is gone."

"No sweat," I said. "I have a good idea who took it, and I think I might know why, too."

I grabbed Mac by her arm and led her quickly back outside. "Now what do we do?" she wanted to know.

"We're going back to the police station and check out those videotapes from the morning Madame Epstein-Hopper bought the farm."

"But we just spent hours looking at them," she complained as I rushed her across the carré Beaumarchais."

"I thought something wasn't quite right about them. And if I remember correctly, you felt the same way."

"Yes, but . . ."

"We can't just sit around and wait for that dinner barge to get back."

We reached the police station and ran up the cement steps to the main entrance. Henri Beauchamp, the sergeant on duty, remembered us. Thanks to LeSeur and Juliette, we were VIPs now, so he had no problem with setting up the tapes again and letting us run them.

We didn't know what we were looking for, of course, but at least now we knew there *had* to be something. The tapes weren't just plain videos after all; they were Dr. Hopper's "iron-clad" alibi. If he'd killed his wife like we knew he did, he'd have to have altered them somehow.

We didn't pick up anything on tape A, but when we viewed the B tape, I spotted what had been itching at me, as if I'd brushed against poison oak. It was something about the quality of the two tapes that didn't match. I wondered if they were different brands. Different fidelities or speeds. I ejected the tape and checked one against the other. Nope. They were the same brand, and identical in every way.

"Let's put the first tape back in," Mac said.

We checked a minute of it, then ejected it and put in tape B.

"It's the light," I said.

"Yes," Mac agreed. "The light in the background."

We called Sergeant Beauchamp back in, and asked him if it were possible to enhance the image. "*Mais oui*," he said. "*Certainement. Un moment, s'il vous plait.*" He hurried off.

"I think he was telling us to hold our horses," I said.

A few moments later, he was back with a rolling table containing another, specialized videotape player, one with console of controls that allowed the viewer to adjust the zoom or alter the lighting and color balance. He set it up, then left again.

"Okay," I said, "stick tape A in and let's see what we've got." Mackenzie did, and we zoomed in.

At the far end of the hallway was a large plate-glass window, part of which was in the camera's stationary frame. We zoomed in still further on it and saw something no one had noticed before. Something so important that it changed everything about the Hopper case.

"Will you look at that?" Mackenzie crowed.

Outside the plate-glass window, *it was raining!*

I quickly ejected the tape and inserted tape B. Through the plate-glass window, sunshine beamed onto the carpeted hallway floor. Mackenzie turned to me with a dazzling smile. "P.C., these two tapes are from different days!"

There was no doubt about it. Mackenzie was right.

"Remember the newspaper article we read about

Genevieve's death?" I said. "There was a terrible storm the night she was murdered!"

"And that's when Maurice Cardin checked in to the Monte Carlo Grand Hotel!"

"So here's how he did it. He checks in as Maurice Cardin after murdering Genevieve. The next morning at five-thirty, he leaves the room to go on his run."

"Yes . . . ?"

"So *that* tape's made, and ready for him to use later. Then comes the night he kills his wife. Remember, she died between six-thirty and seven A.M."

"Right."

"He kills his wife at, say, six-thirty or a little after. He jogs straight to the café, and chats up the staff till seven, the time the hallway tapes are changed. Then he returns to the hotel, possibly in a disguise, and heads for the security office. Somehow, he finds the tape that's just been taken out of the machine, and switches it with the one from the week before that shows him leaving at five-thirty. Of course, he changes the label on it first, to match up the date. He exits the hotel, ditches his disguise somewhere, and returns to his suite at seven-fifty."

"How did he get into the tape room?"

"He probably swiped the key and made a copy. Everything around here is a little *comme çi, comme ça* anyway."

We sat there for a while in silence. We had our proof. It was now obvious to us that Dr. Hopper *was* indeed

Maurice Cardin. We knew what he'd done, and how he'd done it.

When the sergeant came in again, we tried our best to convey this information to him, but either we were too excited to make any sense, or his English was not too swift. He ended up calling in another officer to talk to us. We explained to both of them what we'd found, and showed them the mismatch on the videotapes. They finally understood, but neither officer had the authority to issue a warrant for Dr. Hopper's arrest.

Sergeant Beauchamp phoned Dijon, and was on the horn for some time, growing more and more frustrated, his voice rising as he tried and failed to locate the Dijon chief inspector in what had to be a legal and media circus following the Cyrano arrest. Finally, Beauchamp hung up. "I am most sorry," he told us. "But they confirmed that Inspector LeSeur is on a plane coming back to Monaco, but there is no transmission just now. We'll have to wait another hour or so."

"But Hopper could be out of the country by then!" Mackenzie protested.

"Can't you at least take him in for questioning?" I pressed.

"I am sorry," the sergeant said. "Regulations, you understand?"

"Not really," I said, and grunted.

"Come on, P.C.," Mackenzie said, dismissing them all. "There's no sense in hanging around here. Let's go find Hopper ourselves and keep an eye on him until Inspector LeSeur can order these *gendarmes* to get their act together. But you know," she added, as we went back outside and a night mist from the Mediterranean washed over us, "we still can't be certain Francine White wasn't in this thing with him. With Hopper. What do we say if we run into the two of them?"

I thought that one over a moment. "Well," I finally said, "I suppose we just say, 'Oh, hello. We're here to baby-sit you until the posse arrives, but say—what's it like to be a pair of cornered homicidal maniacs in love?'"

12

The Last and Most Desperate Meeting

We left the police station in a huff, and headed back toward the dock. The boat was still out on the cruise. The staff at the dock told us it wouldn't be back for at least another hour. It was now almost nine-thirty. "I don't know about you," I told Mackenzie, "but I'm about ready for some dessert."

"Mmm," she said. "I agree. Stuffing our faces with comfort food is definitely called for."

We headed back to Le Bon Appétit. It was well after dark now, and the place was crowded. All the sidewalk tables were taken, and it was only by sheer coincidence that we got our old table back. We ordered a gooey crème brûlée and congealed raspberry crepes from the selection the waiter presented to us. We both had two café au laits to go with our splurge. Mac tried dialing Juliette, but the phone only made a freaky noise.

"How about we call Jesus?" I suggested.

"Okay." Mackenzie handed me the phone.

I punched in the number and waited while the phone

rang and rang. Finally, Jesus' voice came on the line. *"Hola?"*

"Jesus, it's me—P.C.," I said.

"Hey, bro'. What's up?"

"I have some news." I paused for effect. "We found out who killed Dr. Epstein-Hopper!"

"No way! Who was it?"

"It was her husband. We've got proof! The guy faked his alibi. He substituted an earlier surveillance video for the one taken that morning. His shrink girlfriend who looks like Alice B. Toklas may be in on it, too, but I doubt it."

"Nice going, P.C. Did the police arrest him yet?"

"No. They're waiting to get the orders from higher up. But Dr. Hopper is *toast*. Mac and I are going to stake him out until the police get it together."

"Hey, be careful, man."

"Will do. Thanks. *Ciao* for now, baby. We'll let you know how it goes down."

We hung up, and I handed the cell phone back to Mac. As I did, I noticed a guy in a black raincoat getting up from a sidewalk table not far away. The man had his back to us and had been half-hidden by a glittering belle époque sculpture. There was something about the urgency with which he moved that caught my attention. "Hey, Mac," I whispered.

"Omigod," she said, as the man scurried like a rodent across the boulevard toward our hotel. "It's Hopper!"

"He must have overheard me," I said. "Holy kamozes, I just assumed he was on that cruise boat!"

"Come on!" she said, already running.

I followed right behind her, ignoring the angry shouts of the waiter, who had his hands full of steaming coffee cups and gluttonous plates of pastries. Once again, we'd flown the coop, and this time, without paying. Right now, we had bigger fish to fry.

We sprinted into the lobby, but there was no sign of Hopper. "What do we do now?" Mac asked.

"He might have gone up to his suite," I said.

"Do you think he overheard you talking to Jesus?"

"Must have," I said. "Try calling Juliette again."

Mac whipped out her cell phone, while I tried to figure out what to do. I guessed we were better off staying down in the lobby. That way, if he tried to make a break for it, we'd be more likely to spot him and less likely to cross paths on the elevators. Besides, if he decided to get violent or try any of his pillow tricks on us, well, at least there would be witnesses.

"Still no luck!" Mackenzie cried in frustration, folding up her cell phone and stuffing it back into her daypack.

Suddenly, through the slab of glass windows to the left of the lobby, I'd spotted a black BMW roadster coming down the driveway. A valet got out of it, and was tipped—by Hopper! As we watched, he threw a suitcase into the car, got in, and started to drive off like a Grand Prix racer.

"He's making a break for it!" I shouted. "Come on!"

We dashed for the revolving doors. Outside, we saw the BMW pulling out into the traffic of the place du Casino, and heading east down the boulevard.

"Egad!" I said. "We've got to follow him!"

We looked at the line of people waiting for cabs in front of the hotel. "Not gonna happen," Mackenzie said.

I scanned the curb and saw a motor scooter with a sidecar parked nearby. The driver was nowhere in sight, but whoever it was had left the keys in the ignition. "Follow me!" I yelled, breaking into a run. I straddled the scooter, and motioned for Mackenzie to hop into the sidecar. "We'll explain later."

"Yes, when we're locked up," she said as I turned the key and gunned the motor. "I think this constitutes major theft. And I read the French prisons have rats the size of alley cats!"

We could still make out the Beemer stopped at a traffic light up ahead. But Hopper must have spotted us in his rearview mirror, because all of a sudden, he made a screeching U-turn around the divider, and headed west, passing us to our left!

The light was about to turn green, and once the boulevard traffic got going, I knew it would take forever to make that U-turn. So I didn't wait. I guided the scooter up onto the grassy divider and cut right over into the westbound lanes before the traffic caught up to us.

The scooter bounced all over the place and skidded back and forth with Mackenzie screaming before I finally regained control. A moment more and we were back in the chase, just a hundred yards or so behind Hopper.

"You maniac!" Mackenzie shouted at me over the roar of the engine. "I should never have let you drive!"

"Hey, you're still alive, aren't you?" I shot back. I kept the pedal to the metal, zigzagging between cars to keep the Beemer in sight.

"Hey, get us closer! I could phone in the license number. We could use a little police backup, you know."

"Good idea!" I was trying, goodness knows. But BMW's are built for speed, and solid as our little Vespa was, we were losing ground, not gaining. It was only the slower traffic in front of Hopper that was keeping us from losing him altogether. We could weave between the cars, he couldn't.

The Beemer took a right turn, and shot up into the cutbacks of the hills—heading in the direction of Nice. And the airport! Here on the cliffside corniche road, there was less traffic, and we were starting to lose sight of Hopper whenever he rounded a bend.

Finally, we lost him altogether. We were alone on the road, with only the occasional car coming our way in the other lane. There was nobody ahead of us for as far as we could see. I pulled the scooter over. "He's gone," I said with a heavy sigh. "Now what?"

"We catch him at the airport," Mac yelled, exasperated.

"Even if we did, how could we stop him from getting on a plane? And he may not be heading for the airport after all. Maybe he's just driving to some hideout."

Mac began to slap the side of the bucket she was sitting in, as if it were a bad pony.

I swung us around, and we started heading back toward Monaco. "I suppose we'd better return this scooter, too," I yelled over the din of the motor. "Before we get ourselves arrested. We can't do much good if we're locked up behind bars."

We were now on the cliff side of the road, and the view of the coast was totally spectacular and perilous. "We really should stay away from cliffs," Mac was shouting as we passed a dirt side road on our left. There came the sound of a powerful engine roaring into action, and the Beemer came darting out at us, its high beams crashing into my mirrors and blinding me for a moment. I had to swerve to avoid being slammed into, and knocked straight off the cliff. Mac was screaming like a banshee now, and I guess I was, too. I was too busy trying to keep control of the scooter to notice.

I gassed the scooter, but the Beemer swung in behind our tail—and it was gaining on us like a T. rex.

"Go right!" I heard Mac shout, so I did, first faking left to throw Hopper off. It bought us a couple of seconds, but then I heard the screeching of brakes and could see he'd stopped his car on a dime, threw it into reverse, and was after us again.

"Call the police, quick!" I squawked, my voice breaking. Just as Mac flipped open her cell phone, it rang.

"Mayday!" she yelled at the caller. "Emergency! Heeelllp! Heeeeeeelllp!"

Hunting Grounds

"Juliette? Oh, thank goodness it's you!"

Mackenzie shouted into the phone like a hyperventilating chimp as I maneuvered the scooter down the Royal Road. I could still see the Beemer, but with all the hairpin turns, Hopper couldn't really make up any ground on us. We'd gotten close enough for Mackenzie to make out his license number, and she screamed it to Juliette before they were cut off.

"She and her dad are landing in Nice right now," Mac told me.

"Good," I said.

I figured, with a name like Royal Road, we'd be heading for the prince's palace, with all its armed guards on duty. I was determined to keep going, making no turns, but we came to another fork in the road.

I turned right again. Instead of winding up at the palace, the road dead-ended in front of a dark, huge, and deserted stone building with a sign that read INSTITUT OCÉANOGRAPHIQUE.

"Great," I commented, screeching to a halt and

getting off the scooter. "Well, we've been wanting to come here all along, and now, here we are."

"You are weird," Mackenzie grumbled, hopping out of the sidecar just as the Beemer bore down on us. "Now what?"

"Well, it looks to me like there's only one way to go," I said, referring to a ramp that ran along the cliffside edge of the building. To go any other way would mean running right by the BMW. I didn't know if Hopper was armed, but I knew he was desperate and dangerous.

We took the ramp. It ran around the building, climbing slowly. As we ran, we yelled in vain for a watchman to come and help us. "Guess they can't afford night watchmen these days," Mackenzie commented.

Hopper was following us. I couldn't see him, but I could hear him running. He was older than we were, and slower, especially since we were going uphill. But that wasn't going to matter in the end, since we soon found that the ramp ended at a thick plate-glass door. To our left was a steep drop down to sharp, dark boulders and the crashing waves of the Mediterranean. To our right, the ghostly stone bulk of the institute.

Hopper was just coming into view, wheezing and snarling his way up the ramp. Even in the semidarkness, I could see that there was murder in his eyes.

I turned to Mackenzie, and we exchanged a brief glance like dead men walking. Suddenly, she grabbed her boot, yanked it off, and shoved her hand inside it.

She smacked the glass door so hard that it shattered. I kicked in the rest of it with my sneakers, while she put her boot back on. "God bless your sense of fashion, Mac," I said as we stepped through the hole in the door, and into the eerie darkness of the Institute.

We saw a staircase ahead of us. We took it to the second floor and ran down a long hallway, past amazing dioramas of coral reefs and tidal pools. There were phenomenal exhibits of sea upheavals, and skeletons and taxidermy of enormous squid, eels, and predator fish. One whole room was the history of oceanic exploration, wrecks, and treasures. We went up another flight of stairs at the far end of the hallway.

We could hear Hopper on a ramp below us. Mackenzie and I had to stop, unable to speak, and suck in air. My lungs felt like they were going to implode.

We were on a metal walkway, designed like scaffolding, that was halfway up the wall of a vast annex that was the Institute's aquarium. Behind us was a huge window of a colossal tank filled with hammerhead sharks, gliding manta rays, and six-foot-wide Japanese crabs. One after the other, monstrous creatures came within a couple of feet of us, their dark, deadly eyes seeming to stare at us through the thick glass.

The tank gave off a ghastly blue light that flooded the long, high-ceilinged hall and made our skin the color of cadavers we've seen in Mac's mother's morgue. Through the metal grating floor of the ramp, we could make out Hopper on the level below us. He was bent over double, breathing as hard as we were.

After a few moments, he straightened himself, and stared up at us, his eyes narrowed. The look was the same look that was in the eyes of the sharks.

"It's over, Dr. Hopper. Kaput," I said, finally recovered enough for me to speak. "You're not going to get away with any of it. We've already given our evidence to the police. They're looking for you at the border crossings and airports. By this time you couldn't even charter a single-engine Piper Cub if you wanted to." It was all a lie, of course, but I had to try *something*.

There was a snort and a faint rustling, as if a large snake were carefully coiling beneath us. "And what's this so-called evidence you seem to think you have?" His voice was soft, spookly, like a child whispering.

I glanced at Mackenzie, and saw that she was feeling her way along the wall beyond the aquarium window. I knew she was trying to find an alarm or a light switch. Trying to buy us some time, I launched into our case. "I understand why you tried to make it look as though Cyrano had murdered your wife," I said. "But you messed up rather badly."

"Oh, really?" Hopper said, with chillingly unexpected amusement. "How was that?"

"First there was your e-mail slipup."

"Eh?"

"Cyrano's e-mails were all sent in red. But, of course,

you had no way of knowing this because you ripped off all your data on Cyrano from Francine White's notes about the case—didn't you? And since her notes were downloaded in text format, they wouldn't have shown in what color the original e-mails were created."

I stayed close to Mac. She had found a beveled-oak display case in front of a pool of a vast complex of tanks, one filled with piranha. There was a small bust of Jacques Cousteau, who had made the Institute world famous. We tried to lift the bust off its stand, but it was bolted down to foil even the most rabid of tourists.

The little, creepy baby whisper came again from the grating beneath us. "Intriguing," Dr. Hopper said.

I had been fighting it, but fear now begun to grip my throat. Mac picked up on it and took over. "We have to give you an A for effort, Doc," she said. "I mean, coming to Monaco in advance so you could switch the videotapes of the two mornings was brill and bizotic. Too bad it happened to be pouring rain on that first visit. That's the kind of thing you have to watch out for when you do that kind of thing."

Hopper's baby whisper turned into a low, growling sound. Over the edge of the curving ramps we could see him below us, moving toward a display of Eskimo harpoons and skinning equipment.

"And then there's the hair person at Bergdorf's," Mac said. "He'll testify that you made the appointment and were more interested than your wife in the shade of red you were expecting. And the stylist will back him up. . . ."

A laugh came from below. It wasn't raucous or even villainous. It sounded folksy, I thought, as Mac and I saw Dr. Hopper reach for one of the harpoons.

"I applaud your sleuthing," Hopper said. "However, *beauticians for the prosecution* is a rather amusing concept."

"Why did you do it?" I asked. Mac and I were beyond fear now. "Was it Dr. White who convinced you to knock off your wife?"

That got him.

"Francine had nothing to do with this!" he shouted, and I believed him. "Leave her out of it. It was all my idea. My pain of living with my selfish, cold wife for far too many years. She wouldn't let me get a divorce without taking me for every penny I'm worth. She was a selfish, jealous witch, and she was never interested in my career. She was a pathological egotist, and my enemy. Everything I ever achieved was in spite of her, not because of her."

He was staring up from us now at a bend in the ramp, using the staff of the harpoon like a cane. It had what looked like a twelve-inch arrow of metal strapped to the end of it, a piercing tool that looked like a thick home-made butcher knife.

"And Genevieve Blanc?" Mackenzie blurted out. "What did she do to deserve getting murdered?"

A strange smile had frozen onto Hopper's face, as if he were in pain or about to scream. "Too bad about her," he said. "She was a sacrifice. I needed her to cover my tracks, to make the whole shebang look like it was part of a Cyrano rampage. She just happened to have red hair like Harriet. She was an easy, mousy target."

"You killed a total stranger," I said. "In cold blood. Hey, Mac, do they still use the guillotine to execute murderers in France?

"Don't concern yourself with that," Hopper said. "I won't be going to prison. No one's going to arrest me. Not even if, as you say, you've already gone to the police with your so-called evidence. Because I'm not going to be caught."

He made a dash for the stairs up to the third level, and we charged off in the other direction, trying to put as much distance between us and him as possible. "We've got to get out of this mausoleum!" Mackenzie called out to me as we ran.

We ran until we found a staircase, but it dead-ended at the second floor. We emerged into another large hall, this one with huge stuffed killer and humpback whales suspended by wires from the ceiling.

We slunk along the side of the shadowy hall. We passed several small platforms about ten feet off the floor, with metal stairs leading up to them. On the platforms were displayed various submersibles: diving saucers and bathyspheres from Cousteau's early oceanographic expeditions. The bathyspheres were spherical steel containers with thick glass portholes and heavy metal hatches. They were the earliest deep-sea submersibles, allowing humans their first glimpses of the ocean floor.

We reached the far end of the hall and tried the doors. They were locked from the other side. "Come on, P.C.!" Mackenzie said in a hoarse whisper. "We've got to get out the way we came in!"

We were about halfway back down the hall, when the far doors clanged open. Hopper was silhouetted by the blue aquarium lights, searching the darkness ahead of him for any sign of us.

I glanced up at one of the bathyspheres. I silently pointed to it. Mackenzie got the idea, and we climbed the metal stairs to the platform as silently as we could. We slipped inside the bathysphere through the open hatch, then pulled it almost shut behind us, hoping we hadn't been seen. Maybe Hopper would think the whale room was empty, and move on.

It was so dark inside the tiny submersible that all I could see of Mackenzie was the whites of her eyes. I could feel her trembling, and hear her breathing.

Suddenly, *CLANG!*

The hatch was slammed shut. We heard the sound of rusty metal being screwed so tight it squeaked! Through the now-sealed hatch, we could make out Dr. Hopper's appalling laughter. I looked through the single porthole of the sphere and saw him peering in at me, the expression on his face like someone demented.

He grabbed a hose funnel and put it to his mouth. We heard the dreadful, echoing sound of his voice as he spoke to us through it. "It's been nice knowing the two of you," he said. "Sorry I can't stay any longer, but really, that's your own fault. On the chance that you really *did* alert the police, it's best I get going."

My breathing grew more labored by the second as the little air inside the bathysphere began to run out. Mackenzie was already gasping. Hopper kept staring in at us, fascinated by the sight of us growing weaker.

"P.C. . . ." I heard Mackenzie whisper.

"What, Mac?" I replied, my thinking growing fuzzier with each passing moment.

"When I count to three, shove everything you've got against that door."

"Gotcha."

"One, two, THREE!" We slammed ourselves up against the door of the bathysphere. Through the window, I saw Hopper flinch. His eyes widened as he realized what was happening, but it was too late. The huge metal ball with us inside it rocked, and with a second lunge from us, it was *rolling*. We rolled along the short platform, then dropped over the edge. I hit my head hard on the metal wall of the bathysphere and Mackenzie landed on top, knocking the wind completely out of me.

14

A Royal Flush

I had been aware of several bumps as the bathysphere rolled. I knew it had bounced down a few steps and, through the porthole, I caught glimpses of it crashing through the platform railing—but it was all like peering out from a washing machine in the spin-dry cycle. I've only had the wind knocked out of me a few times in my life, but each time it felt like I had an elephant sitting on me and I was going to die. I tried to breathe, but for several seconds no air would fill my lungs.

When it finally did, I cried out, "Mac!"

She pushed herself up off of me, getting her weight off my chest. I was thankful she looked very alive and twitching, and a second later I was with her trying to figure out where the bathysphere had halted. Nearly all the oxygen was gone, and we scampered frantically inside the shadowy death sphere. I joined her pounding on the little round window. A face loomed over us. At first I thought it was Hopper reaching down toward us with a spray of knives. But there came the squeaking sounds of metal on metal again.

The hatch opened, and we were staring into the face of a redheaded angel. We saw that it was Juliette. She and her dad helped us shimmy up out of the hatchway like limp worms oozing up out of a big apple. "What . . . What are you doing here?" I asked. "How'd you find us?"

"You triggered silent alarms all over," LeSeur said.

Juliette reached out and touched our faces, as though to make certain we were both in one piece. "When I had called you, you were driving—turning into the Royal Road. It did not take a genius to put the two things together."

The whole of the museum room was bathed in the stroboscopic lights from a crescent of police cars outside. Their pulsing roof lights flooded everything, and the static and voices on the police radios were like music to our ears. Several policemen were rolling the bathysphere to one side, while a couple of other officers dragged a groaning Dr. Hopper out from between it and the base of a display case of preserved hatchet fish and gulper eels.

"My leg . . . my leg . . ." Hopper was groaning.

"Dr. Hopper—he's . . ."

"Yes, we know. Thanks to you," Juliette said. "He is the killer of his wife and Genevieve Blanc."

"And he has a broken leg thanks to you and Mackenzie," LeSeur told us as he cuffed Hopper. Hopper was lifted, screaming, onto a stretcher and carried out under the watchful eyes of the room full of dead, stuffed fish.

I tried to get up, but the room started spinning around. "Easy, P.C.," Juliette warned me. "Your head has a bump. You must rest with your feet in the air awhile."

I couldn't help smiling, even though my head was killing me. Mackenzie got up with a little assist from Inspector LeSeur. "You are heroes, all three of you!" he exclaimed. He and several of the cops applauded and stamped their feet for Mac, me, and Juliette. The three of us had to laugh.

"I really thought we were gonna die in that thing," Mac complained, running her fingers like a comb through her hair.

"You are safe now," LeSeur said. "And all of Monaco and France are safe from Cyrano and his copycat, thanks to you."

We didn't get to sleep till about three, and even though we're usually early risers, we didn't wake up until ten-thirty the next morning. We would have slept even later, but Mackenzie's dad woke us up to tell us that Juliette was there to see us.

"Hopper, he is in the hospital, under police guard," she informed us. "When he is better, he will go to prison. I do not think he will come out again."

"I sure hope not!" Mackenzie said. "Life's tough

enough without having a ghoul like him walking the streets."

Juliette had other news. "They catch Tomas Milano in Portofino! The Italian carabinieri. They send him back here. I think he, too, is on his way to prison for a long time. And the French prison, it is not like your American prisons. No gourmet chefs. No TV. No personal stereos."

Dr. Riggs came into the living room from his bedroom, rolling a king-size suitcase. "Well, I'm all set to go home. How about you kids?"

"Dad," Mackenzie said. "I thought we didn't have to leave till this afternoon!"

"I just don't want us to miss the plane."

"We have time to hang out with Juliette awhile, don't we?"

"Sure," he said. "Long as you don't go water skiing or parasailing. That's some lump you've got on your head there."

"Souvenir of Monaco," I quipped.

"I want to check out the Oceanographic Institute for real," Mackenzie said. "Those piranha and shark tanks were awesome!"

"Okay," I agreed, "as long as we skip those bathyspheres and stick to the aquarium."

By five-thirty P.M., after a day of hanging out with Juliette, we were all packed and ready to go. We headed down to the lobby so Mac's dad could check us out of our suite. When we stepped off the elevator and into the lobby, there were a couple of hundred people waiting for us. Flashbulbs started going off. Everyone was cheering me, Mac, and Juliette. There were photographers, Inspector LeSeur, and a dozen cops—a whole contingent of the shrink conventioneers!—and lots of staff, and guests. There were what looked like plain old Monegasque folks, too.

I knew from the guidebook that the lobby of the hotel was often used for concerts and public honors. When Princess Grace was alive, she'd even give poetry readings for the guests right smack outside the casino doors near the dozens of racks of postcards of the Royal Family. You were supposed to listen to the Princess or the concert, and then be really fired-up to buy oodles of postcards. It was a little weird, but sort of nice and cultural.

The manager of the hotel peeled the three of us away from Dr. Riggs and led us toward a microphone where an elderly man, impeccably dressed and looking vaguely familiar from the postcards, was waiting for us. He reached out, shook our hands, and kissed us on both cheeks. It felt a little like we were visiting a really high-class Santa Claus at Macy's during Christmas.

"I wish to congratulate you," the distinguished old man said. You will always be honored and welcomed here in Monaco. Our people are forever grateful to you for the bravery and wisdom of your youth, which has put an end to the reign of terror of Cyrano in Paris and the terrible killings here on the Riviera. The three of you are an inspiration to us all, and it is with profound admiration that, on behalf of my grateful country, I present you with the keys to our Principality."

An aide stepped forward with a black-satin tray upon which were three ribbons with silver medals the size of saucers. He placed one around each of our necks, as though we'd just won a very important relay race at the Olympics.

He gave us another bunch of freakazoid cheek-kisses, and there was a repeat explosion of flashbulbs and shutter-clicking like a gaggle of Geiger counters had struck a mother lode. Everyone started clapping madly again.

Prince Rainier stepped back into a flank of aides and bodyguards. His parting words to us were, "I do not say good-bye, but only *au revoir*. We hope to see you again. One day you will dine with us at the palace." He waved and walked very slowly by the racks of Royal Family postcards for sale, then was ducked out the front door into a limo that looked like a custom bulletproof Mercedes the Pope would ride in.

Feeling about as cool as ice cubes, we stepped back into the elevator with Dr. Riggs, LeSeur, and a couple of the bellmen. The applause of the crowd accompanied us until the golden doors slid shut. Me, Mac, and Juliette hugged each other and laughed our heads off as we rode up to the helipad. Dr. Riggs and Juliette's dad looked so proud you'd think they were going to detonate.

Outside on the roof the sun was beginning to dip in the west. Its rays bounced off the Mediterranean, making the sea bluer than we'd ever seen it. Long shadows were cast on the gleaming glass-and-concrete corncob high-rises and lush-terraced mountains.

"We'll never forget you," I told Juliette.

"Come visit us in New York," Mac told her. "You can stay with us for as long as you want."

"Definitely." I seconded the invitation.

"Ah, *oui*. I would love to," Juliette said.

She pressed an envelope into Mac's hand as we hugged a last time. "You will read this on the plane, please," Juliette said. "I hope it amuses you."

The blades of the helicopter had begun to whirl and make it impossible to hear. We bid farewell to Inspector LeSeur. To tell you the truth, we didn't want to leave and go back to Westside School.

"Come on," Dr. Riggs said as he led Mac and me up the ramp into the huge passenger chopper. Soon we were strapped in waving like crazy to Juliette and her dad as the helicopter lifted roaring off the pad. We waved to them until the chopper turned and swung off like a plump red-and-black wasp toward Nice and the airport.

"Well," I shouted over the noise of the rotors, "another mystery solved. Give me five, partner."

Mac smacked my hand in celebration. We had decided to wait until we had boarded our 757 jet at the Nice airport and were taking off before reading Juliette's letter. Mac used one of her long green-painted fingernails to cut open the envelope. We scanned her words together, and laughed until we were far out over the Mediterranean and heading home:

```
There once was a guy named PC
Who was too smart for Hopper,
            mais oui!
          But PC saw red
Thanks to Mac's tingly head—
Now "Maurice" won't be going
          scot-free!
```

CHECK

OUT

THE

NEXT

P.C. HAWKE

MYSTERY . . .

From the terrifying files of P.C. Hawke:
THE LETHAL GORILLA • Case #4

Mac and I stood transfixed at the entrance to Congo Land and the Gorilla Forest, where it seemed we were peering into a frightening manifestation of Ivan Allen's mind. We knew he had been behind the project, that it was the birth of his imagination—this slab of a jungle wall that stood before us. There were lengths of high, strong metal fencing dressed and hidden with thick impenetrable poles of African bamboo and vines. Over the clumps of massive real and man-made boulders rose a forest of mangroves, balsa, and mimosa trees, a thousand trunks shooting up over a hundred feet high from a maze of half-buried buttresslike roots. The forest's canopy practically blotted out the sun.

The main gate itself was like the gaping mouth of a monstrous viper with two vast, closed wooden doors that looked as if they were holding back a minotaur or a King Kong. The whole facade was something huge and secret and frightening. I took a deep breath as the sound of a motor began to intrude.

Mac and I were startled to look up and see a man

1

descending from the canopy toward us like a pilot with an invisible parachute.

"Egad," I muttered.

"What is this?" Mackenzie asked.

It took a moment before we could understand that the floating human form was in some sort of a wire gondola attached to the end of a long hydraulic arm with collapsible sections like a fishing rod. The base of the arm was the bed of a parked heavy-duty, customized truck.

We watched the man working the control levers in the gondola steer himself out of the jungle. Closer, he looked to be about sixty, was wearing a groundskeeper's uniform, and had a grouchy face, wrinkled like a pink linen suit. As he floated to within twenty feet of us, what struck me most was that the gondola he was in was covered with the same sort of amber specks we'd seen on Ivan Allen's clothes—and I hadn't seen a bit of them anywhere else at the zoo.

"The Congo doesn't open for another hour," the man said, smiling. He must have thought we were just a couple of regular kids visiting the zoo.

"Will we be able to see the gorillas?" Mac asked. She had let her hair down and shook it loose. She always does that whenever she really wants to disarm somebody. "I love gorillas."

"Sure," the groundskeeper said.

"How about the jaguars?" I asked.

"Nope," the man said. The smile faded from his face, but he still looked pretty friendly. "We're working on their moat. You might be able to see them at the end of the day. Maybe tomorrow."

He grasped the gondola's controls and started to guide it away from us and back toward the base of the truck. Mac and I ran after him. "What are all those specks on your bucket?" I called over the whir of the motor. "They look like some kind of sap."

"Yep."

"Our bio and science teachers never told us about trees whose sap runs in the fall," I said, trying to sound like a really mentally challenged student. Mac did a little skip and let out a really inane giggle to help me out. "I don't see any sap on the ground," I added.

The man stopped his gondola right over us. "You get an Indian summer like this one, and the tops of the mangroves and mimosas think it's spring. The canopy gets a lot of sap."

"Only in the canopy?" Mac asked. "Just those top branches of the forest?"

"Yeah," the man said. He looked ready to grasp the controls again, and then stared at us. "Why'd you ask?"

I decided to go for the full shock value. "Her mom's the Medical Examiner," I said, indicating Mac. "We were just wondering how all the sap specks and smudges got on Ivan Allen's clothes. Were you around when they found the body?"

The man's face hardened into what looked to me to be a mask of anger and hate. I thought he was going to spit on us, but instead he looked back toward the outer jungle of Congo Land as if we no longer existed. He squeezed his control sticks and the hydraulic valves began to ooze apart and whir him back over the fence and up toward the treetops. I was going to yell something after him just to make him really nuts, but there was the sound now of sirens and a gaggle of cop cars pulling onto the zoo grounds. Three patrol cars with lights flashing came right down the roadway and pulled into a service road that circled around the back of Congo Land.

"Something's happened," I said. "Let's get back."

As we hurried up the main path, returning the way we'd come, I yanked my cell phone out and punched in Mrs. Riggs's cell number. "What's up, Kim?" I said. She likes us all to just call her Kim, so I do it. Mac made me stop near the Dancing Crane Café so she could jam her ear next to mine and listen, too.

"We've got a crime scene," Mrs. Riggs said. "You'd better get back here pronto."

"What?" Mac yelled into the receiver.

"What'd you find out about the blood?" I asked. I knew it had to have something to do with that. "It's the blood, right?"

"Yeah," Mrs. Riggs said.

If the zoo had been declared a crime scene, both

Mackenzie and I knew what the crime had to be. "You think someone murdered Ivan? Is that what you think now? Someone deliberately gave him the wrong kind of blood?"

"Bingo."

"How do you know it wasn't an accident?" I asked. "Maybe the labels just got mixed up. He was type A. What type did they give him?"

"Gorilla," Mrs. Riggs said, sounding really weirded-out.

"Gorilla?" Mac said, shocked.

"Yes," Mrs. Riggs clarified. "Nice, fresh gorilla blood."

P.C. HAWKE mysteries

MORE P.C. HAWKE MYSTERIES COMING SOON!

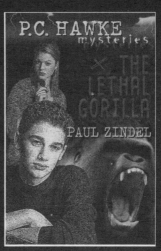

#4: THE LETHAL GORILLA

A scientist at the Bronx Wildlife Conservation Park turns up dead, and P.C. and Mackenzie are sure it's no accident.

Available October 2001

Read more about P.C. Hawke at www.pchawke.com

AN IMPRINT OF HYPERION BOOKS FOR CHILDREN